VERDANT GROUNDS SUBTLE BOUNDARIES

VERDANT GROUNDS SUBTLE BOUNDARIES

A Collection of Short Stories By

ANDERS M. SVENNING

Adelaide Books
New York / Lisbon

2017

VERDANT GROUNDS, SUBTLE BOUNDARIES
A Collection of Short Stories
By Anders M. Svenning

Published by Adelaide Books, New York / Lisbon
An imprint of the Istina Group DBA
adelaidebooks.org

Editor-in-Chief
Stevan V. Nikolic

Cover Design & Book Formatting: Istina Group DBA

For any information, please address Adelaide Books
at info@adelaidebooks.org

ISBN13: 978-0-9995164-0-9
ISBN10: 0-9995164-0-X

Printed in the United States of America

Contents

Planes

Not long after the plane lands, Davis Parker finds himself behind the wheel of his aged and misshapen Lincoln Town Car. Road lights coast past, methodical, casting feigning shadows across the dashboard, which has his eyes strained even more so than his jet lag.

It is something he has grown used to, the fatigue. It comes along with his profession; and it has been said by a considerable few—scientists, theorists, and psychologists—that commercial pilots experience shorter life spans as an effect of the detrimental lack of sleep, numbers ranging from as early as one's mid-fifties, the causes of death a disingenuous slew from heart attacks to quiet exits in one's sleep to death not of the body but of the mind.

All that, though, in the words of Dave Parker's woman, is mere statistics. Jessie would be curled up in bed, waiting for the morning and her husband's company with expectations of late night popcorn and candlelit dinners coloring her dreams. "Statistics," she says, "shouldn't be regarded as anything more than numbers and false positives. You just can't trust those numbers, you know?" That is her gift to him. Besides her surprise evening kabobs and the lessening-in-frequency in-shower involvements, that is her gift to him—wisdom and council—given through by the shade of her charm, a gift to her otherwise "dense but heartfelt husband," unable to separate hype from truth. "It's all about how you live your life, you know? Munch on fast food on your layovers and you're going to have a heart attack. It's that simple." And it is that simple.

Simple, just like—altitude. Everything is relative. Yet still, the notion of numbers and studies holds-fast in Davis's mind at inopportune times, thirty thousand feet in the air, listless.

A cup of coffee has been drank just after his landing in Miami, bitter and burnt; but it is something to keep him occupied from passing out standing up or passing out driving, like a narcoleptic. It did not have much taste at all, the coffee; Davis has been up for what is now nearing thirty-six hours, and his senses, he knows, tend to dull when he hits hour twenty-four, if not hour twenty, thanks to countless cups of the stuff and caffeinated sodas. Now, there is only the drive home, then he can shoot headfirst under the sheets for hibernation.

Alignment needs fixing. The car, a 1999 piece of work, color white, with glossy hubcaps, is still chuffing along, a beater, in all respects, enough to get him from the house to the airport and back, dinged, incognito, and grand. The Lincoln feels cheap to Davis after landing such a behemoth of an aircraft. It is a good transition, though, from that preciseness to the ease of home life. Davis stays course northward toward Boca Raton, high-speed vibrations jarring loose attentiveness, shaking him into trance.

Loose fitted clothing, long hours in the sky, nothing

more than a dim overhead light, enough to read a book. The drone of four low-humming jet engines, the intimacies of the flight and in effect the ride home. Light sandwiches and orange juice from the cockpit cooler; red, green, and white luminescence on the console before him, countless switches, buttons, gauges and dials, levers, static and radio frequencies.

It used to be a passion, breathing inside the clouds, pulling Cessna's noses up into a loop, feeling his lips, cheeks, and forehead rescind the direction of the plane, carrying the weight of the centripetal forces, extending the flaps of the small turbo-prop and opening up the window to stick out his hand and scoop the air like ice cream.

It was a childhood dream, flying, and flying never quite lost its exhilaration even as a captain of the seven-fifty- and seven-sixty-seven, especially during takeoff: a wild ferocity under the sweaty, expectant hand of just as well many pilots before his. And still, flying is not quite the same as the early days, in the small planes, when he knew nothing separated him from the ground but fiberglass and water vapor. Jessie has grounded him, her heart and home-style cooking an endless well of flavor and smells. Davis Parker has speculated how, even through her impeding bangs, she notices the flaws in his evening dress or the spot of tomato sauce on his chin during dinner.

Familiar clusters of trees and road-signs tell Parker he is nearing his exit. Vibrations escalate to fervent jostling at around fifty-five miles per hour, settle back to a comfortable streamline at forty.

The three-way intersection of Grevillea Lane and

Shoreline Road is not far off. He would make the left onto Grevillea presently and would strip down to essentials upon climbing the stairs, casting aside the clothing's mundane represent-ation of the past fourteen days in Germany and flights reaching as far south and east as Dubai, UAE, then crawl into bed for a very much anticipated sleep.

His ear is bitten almost clean off that night. The thing should have burst, the way she has bitten into it. After two cranberry and vodkas each, they are red hot, piping, and her smoky eyes have sent him to the floor. He has found what he needed to catch his second wind—alcohol, women—she has been planning this surprise for days, this swirling ease and rock, sunburst cycles between strength and nurture.

Five hours later, morning is creeping in through the half-slit Venetian blinds; dew clings to the glass. The sunlight is laid like a quilt over Davis and has him dressed to the effect of a grocery store loaf of bread: a striped sun-and-shadow barcode draped over his body. Sleep when you're dead.

He swings out his body, shuffles to the master bath, and brushes his teeth in his own sink for the first time in weeks. He can smell the bright fruity Kenyan organic breathing from downstairs, Jess's favorite, the Kenyan. It is almost too sunny this morning, Davis squinting through the silver sunlight, and walking downstairs.

Jess is already in her solid yellow sundress, floats across the tile floor into her husband's arms when he emerges. "Coffee's up, Dave. Welcome home!" She pecks him a kiss and floats back toward the kitchen table. "I took the liberty of making you some toast. I've already had breakfast." The beige grout glows from between the tiles underneath Davis's feet. The entire room is glowing, the blue morning light, the walls around him suggesting a definitive break from the outside world and the inside world. The house is florescent—the alcohol, maybe, from last night, he thinks. The sex? Davis pours himself a coffee and has a seat across his wife, the steam still rising from the mug, and the two are quiet for a moment, feeling the pressure and vibrations lingering from the previous night.

"How've you been," Davis asks. "You seem happy, to say the least."

"How couldn't I be?" she replies. "I've been sleeping like a baby recently. I don't know why. Oh, and Beth and I went to the ocean the other night to watch the meteor shower." Davis raises his eyebrows from behind his coffee. "It was beautiful, but I'm sure you see meteors all the time."

"We see some."

"We saw a bunch. And the wine. It makes them have some kind of meaning, you know? Like they really are wishes."

"How is Lillian?"

"She's doing well," says Jess.

"Where is she anyway, sleeping?"

"Sleeping upstairs still."

"I'll be right back." Davis lifts his weight from his seat, coffee in hand, and returns to the bedroom.

Somewhere deep down in the luggage lies a large chocolate candy bar wrapped in a white wrapper, in between two magazines he has snagged from an airport kiosk.

Rummaging through the suitcase, brazen sunlight crystallizing the bedroom, he retrieves the chocolate bar and strides, thoughtful, through the upstairs hallway, past the bathroom on the left side and past the tapestry on the right, into his daughter's room.

The yellow walls soften him, and he lulls the eight-year-old child, Lillian, who is maintaining, it seems, her deep meditative state. Lillian, with puffy cheeks and stringy hair, is sleeping on her side with her arm curled into the other and with her legs, he knows, crossed at the ankles. She has been photographed with her ankles crossed three months before her original birthday, vis a vis a sonogram, and she still sleeps the same way at the age of eight years old.

Davis uses his toes to carry him across the room to the side of Lillian's bed and there he stays for a moment as she breathes. Breathing in and out, her eyes flutter open, and her lungs fill with air.

"Hey, Bird," says Davis, his eyes stringent but warm. The chocolate bar rises from behind the bedside, where it has been hidden and where Davis is crouching. Lillian, still in her post-morning state, is anticipating this treasure, for she knows beforehand her father would be home on this morning, and, as her vision came to focus, seeing the chocolate, she sprouts, yelling, "Oh my God! It's the biggest chocolate bar I've ever seen. Dad, is it for me?"

Davis hums, "Is it for you?" Hums again. "This three pound piece of candy from the chocolate center of the world, is it for you? Hmm, well, it can be yours only if—hmm—only if you count to—a baker's dozen."

She begins counting, reciting slow the numbers, to the number twelve.

"And?" Davis says. "And?"

"Dad, please!"

"Okay, Bird, say 'thirteen' and it's yours."

"Mom went to the meteor shower. I didn't go though."

"No problem, Bird, there will be another one in a couple months."

Lillian says, "Thirteen."

"That's a girl. Go ahead and have a piece of chocolate then clean your teeth. I'll meet you downstairs in five."

"Thanks, Daddy." Lillian bounces up and goes to her desk to open the candy bar while Davis returns to the master bedroom to unpack.

The bedroom, as far as he could tell, has not changed since they have moved into the house, the two small Germanic tapestries on the wall above their bed, an arm chair in the corner. The clothes have begun to unpack themselves, the shirts forming a stack on Davis's left, pants stacked beside the shirts, the shoes and toiletries taking their usual spots alongside the edge of the bag where they would stay until next week when he would have to leave again, on another trip.

One addition they have made to the room since the closing is the mirror opposite their bed. A large crystal, bordered by worn blue-painted wood, takes up nice space on the wall. Davis Parker, walking across his room out the door to meet his child and wife downstairs, catches his eye inside it, and is encountered by strange sense of jamais vu, upon seeing his reflection.

When the pilot, Davis Parker, his wife and his daughter arrive at the zoo later that day they find something that cannot be found elsewhere, even in the walls of their home or in the nuts of a chocolate bar. They observe the animals in their habitat. The trees are not indigenous, the rocks are not as real as they should be, the water the animals drink is from a tap, but otherwise it is the same. The animals know no different. Davis Parker himself can see little difference. All places remind him of the same place.

Lillian, in her great innocence in the world, has been adopted, and is not the direct branch from the parents—Davis and Jessie—and the two, Davis and Jessie, decide on keeping the secret well stored in their hearts. The decision has been made before Lillian's birth, months prior of which, when they have the opportunity to see the sonogram. The only people who know Lil is adopted are the two, and that is as confining as keeping the secret locked within their own, though one has never shared the thought with the other.

Lillian knocks on the glass dividing the viewing area from Nairobi, Kenya. A caracal stares bug eyed back at her. The lynx-like cat has triangular tipped ears with black fur and twists its tail as Lillian knocks. It then moves, walks down the path a few feet to where the trail continues up the wall, and the cat laps up water from a cistern with a small sign above it that reads, Leave Water On.

Riding Amtrak, back when working and when the family is living in Virginia, he keeps photos in his wallet, one of Lillian, one of Lillian and Jessie, one of all three of them. The wallet has shrunk over time.

What used to be a leather brick, is now a white sliver with a screen, which shows the high definition pictures of his family, and Boeing seven-fifty- and seven-sixty-sevens, as well as photos of great meals and the past year's Halloween—the carving of the Jack-o-lantern, the costume party—which is Davis's fondest memory between then and now. Davis dresses as Bloody Monster and Jessie dresses in a black leotard and is wearing black wings, which cling weightless to her back. The two have dressed Lillian as a turboprop biplane, the four wings sticking out on either side like extra limbs.

The costume party is to take place at an acquaintance's home, one's home who has been introduced to the Parkers through a man, Charles Osberg, who is also a pilot. Osberg, with his chivalric tone and brown wavy hair, has found a wife and has decided to slow down, to take his time and make money, and create a family, get a better job and travel the world, see the onion tops of the Taj Mahal, the decrepit stones of the Great Wall, and the configured steps up the Andes, which the Incas have seeded. Osberg, on Halloween, has announced he has accomplished most of these benchmarks.

"Yet to have kids though," Charles Osberg says. The ground rumbles and vibrates along with the party guests—the children, the adults, the witches, ghosts, and mummies. Apple bobbing is underway and there is still four bags of apples stashed in the corner away from the bucket. "Yet to have kids," Osberg says again. "Hey, it's not like they're some kind of rare commodity. Too many of them homeless around the world. You should have seen what it was like in Bombay. Ghettos stretching miles. These people run across the runway, Dave, you should see it. They run across the runway when the plane's coming in. Ghetto's right next to the airport. God knows what they're looking for."

"Good food, good times."

"Hey, say that again. Lillian's behind you."

"Lillian, come over here!" shouts Davis. The girl taxies backwards out of the crowd surrounding the punch bowl. The wings have grown clumsy, bumping into tables and people. "Lillian, you remember Mr. Osberg, right?"

"Mr. Osberg? I think so. Yeah, Mr. Osberg!"

"How are you, Lillian? I've been seeing you fly around this party all night. Looks like your having a blast. You're a lucky girl, Lillian, having this guy as your father." Lillian nods; the party hums. "You know what? Yes, you even have his eyes."

"Okay, Charlie," Davis chuffs.

"No, really. You have his eyes, and because of that I know you'll be as good a person as him. I can see these things, Lillian"

"Thanks, Charlie. She's a good girl."

"Seriously, just don't forget who brought you into this world, Lillian. Because if you do, there's no point to this life. You have know where you've been and where you're going. Me? Kuala Lumpur next month." He laughs.

"Kuala Lumpur, huh?" Davis asks. Where you've been, where you're going. "Never been there." The party begins buzzing in his ear, like a mosquito. "Maybe one day, huh, Lillian? Maybe you're on your way to Kuala Lumpur."

The dripping of the punch bowl, the wet faces bobbing for apples. "Never say never, huh, Bird?" No point.

Davis starts noticing the painted-on moles and the green skins of witches with more intensity. He can no longer differentiate who is beneath the rolls and rolls of toilet paper. Dracula's lips are covered in red blood and he is biting into the neck of a woman, who is laughing. The Joan of Arc leans against the wall in her gnarled armor, looking intoxicated. Jessie is over by the stereo, talking with another patron. A long while has passed since the early days, but the times are moving, moving; she is doing well.

He has not told Charles yet that he is getting transferred to the Miami hub, onto being captain of the seven-forty-seven. Virginia has been a good rush. At long last the planes, the largest planes in the world, are in his palms, and at his fingertips. He flies the gargantuan machines into the air, and feels the heaviness, the lift of the aircraft, lifting him into the skies, where he sees the extensive curvature of the earth, and the stenciled coasts and wispy waters of the earth, where he glides across the clouds crocheted at the top of the world, and he thinks, after long, hard work and dedication, With all the bad going on in that world down there, it is really not so bad at all, not so bad at all, all the way up here.

A long, pallid silo juts from between his knuckles. He sits back a moment looking at the Florida starlight. It is a clear night; he has never seen so many stars from his home. It is as if he could pluck one from the sky and pop it into his mouth and taste; they are so vivid.

Humidity low, temperature moderate, visibility ideal, turbines imploding, he feels however facetious. Jessie has almost let it slip. The woman has taken a highway up into dreamland and has almost let it slip. Lillian would have been a mess.

He can understand though. Options are not abundant. Back when they pick her up from the hospital options are not abundant. They have no choice but to adopt; it seems it is not meant to be, them having their own children—Lillian, though, in all senses, in most senses, is their child.

Years of timing and ovulation cycles, countless organic and synthesized supplements, stretching, experimentation, love and hope cannot deem him father of his own child. And he has redoubtable desire. He wishes to see his wife bear a child, he wishes to see her belly grow, he wishes to hold his own child and feel that incomprehensible connection, that connection knowing this child is a part of him, that this child has his blood inside, has his mind and tendencies, his color, his depth and chromosomes and his parents' chromosomes and their parents' chromosomes.

And Jessie has almost let it slip. What is the point? If the child knows, the magic is gone. Belief is a strong emotion, but what happens if she is to know? Would he be less a father? The thought tolls like a bell. It has grown redoubtable. She has almost told Lillian she is adopted.

The stars are keeping Davis's mind taught. Sleeping inside is Lillian in his bed. Jessie is flitting in and out of the bedroom. Davis's hand is trembling.

His coughing is too loud to be subtle. He takes another drag off the cigarette. Grown on a field out west, this is medicinal, and that makes all the difference. He has his permit to smoke this stuff however shunned it may be for pilots. It is an infrequent habit, smoking, and will be out of the system in less than a week, back, ready and sure for work.

He coughs, rancid, inhaling, and returns his wrist to the armrest. Spicy smoke fills his sinuses. Already he can feel his body warming and blood collecting in his eyes, home seeming a softer tone. Now, instead of vividness, the world around him is different, though still the same place. He feels some sort of togetherness with the trees, the railing, the grass, that big ball of cheese in the sky, this seat beneath him, its mesh holding him. He can feel himself rising. Toke. Gray smoke filling his lungs and turns him into vapor. He can feel the space around him as a dome, not the trees far away, but the space around him, his personal space; he can feel himself, all within arms reach. 300 degrees North-North -West, incline of 30 degrees, is Jessie, pink and solid.

The bus stop just short of Maslow Rx. was the first time. Another couple of minutes and they would have been running, trying to catch up with Bus D and end up walking, having a cup of coffee at Lyle's, where they would have their second date, lose their heads, skip town, and go to Mexico for the weekend; but instead they remain tied, shackled, ball and chain, squeezed into two seats on the bus after a quick conversation, and exchanged phone numbers and kisses, and more words, "I'll have you tomorrow," croaked into his ear. The prospect of figuring out how to get her to fix her lips would be a true accomplishment; the fragments of bad times and the fuzz of the good in between them keeps them at bounds. The more the merrier, and the less the more you will have to keep at it, making love, a child, or a midnight snack.

Nothing more can enter his skull but more smoke, and the all-superior notion that this time is his. The two girls inside and the night itself will keep him rolling on, Aurora Borealis in perpetuity, and his little girl, just inside, sleepy enough to miss it; maybe she is the one dreaming it up. Penny-copper hair and graphite eyebrows woven into cream skin, woven into the smoke; those small nostrils she uses to breathe; her bright voice, bright, much too bright to be kept clotted inside that furry mane.

Psychologists say no two people see the world the same way. Davis wonders just how that chocolate bar tasted to his little girl; did she enjoy the dark chocolate more or the nuts? He feels pressure at the top of his head—it happens when he smokes this stuff and tonight he needs it—a beam into the skies past the moon and astral dusts, navigating through the planets and constellations, the rings of Saturn too ill-fit for any woman's finger he has known; he is driven forward, seeing his oblong self blow out of the Milky Way galaxy; the vanilla swirl he knows and loves is shrinking. Home. He does not know where he has been going, where his family is. Past the boundless expanse he slows.

He is tranquil, suspended and floating in space, with nothing surrounding him. All there is to know, here, is a wide space available to breathe, and it is his, this incredible airiness, this incomprehensible reality. And he feels that familiar sensation—home. He turns an outward eye further away, but can see blackness, blackness in all directions.

There is no difference no matter which way he looks. The blackness can go on forever. Before the day starts, he almost feels the charged weight of the world descending on him, the cushion of his bed and sheets, and it is gone just as he wakes, unattainable.

Days in the sky, and the world is the same, the whole world a simple jump away. He takes one final toke and is burned by the filter's heat; it has been smoked down so close. Not just the opening of the glass door jounces him but his daughter's sigh as well from inside, and he rises, flicks the non-existent cigarette over the balcony rail, and returns into his bedroom.

The pink and blue checked coverlet is wrapped around little Lillian like a roll. The little pink piglets of her toes are poking from the open ends. He, nonsensical, accepts that this is his and this is what he made his life up to be, a caricature of locales around the world, as if the little tokens he brings home capture the outlandish reality of their respective birthplaces.

"Let's get her to bed."

Davis flinches, having forgot he is not alone, that Jess is there. "I'll get her." The smoke clings to his shirt. "Little girl, are you ready to go to your own bed? Lil?" A nod of her head and extended arms tells Davis and his apparition of a wife that she is quite ready for bed.

"Good, Lil, come on." Quick and purposeful steps draw the two closer to the girl's yellow walled room. Davis is quick in putting her to bed, so that she does not get too roused and wake them up at three A.M. "Good night, Lillian. I'll see you tomorrow. Pleasant dreams—"

"How was she?"

"Out like a light."

"Fantastic. Are you tired?"

"Not quite," Davis says, crawling under the covers. The bed is still warm where Lillian has been sleeping.

"You know you are a good father."

"She almost found out tonight that I'm not her father at all, thanks to you."

"I didn't say anything."

"You would have if I didn't shove that sugar cookie in your mouth. What were you thinking?"

"She has to find out some day," says Jess. "Just—"

"Just let it happen naturally."

"That's how I do things. Naturally," says Jess, her nails caressing Davis's arm. "It wouldn't have been so bad."

"Not so bad for you."

"Dave, stay quiet. Quiet your mind. Pretend you're in an airplane." Davis senses a change in air pressure. "Pretend we're in an airplane together. Does it get cold in the cockpit?"

"Sometimes."

"Pretend we're in a cockpit," says Jess. "Pretend we're the only ones in the cockpit."

"Not hard to do."

"Pretend I'm the airplane. Take me somewhere, Dave," caressing his chest. "Take me somewhere," pinching his nipple.

Vessels dilated, influx at one-hundred percent, the descent is definite. Tweaking one side, she raises his shirt and traces clouds into his chest. "Pretend we're over the

Antarctic," bending and nibbling each nipple. And descending.

"How about Africa," Davis says. "I've never been to Africa."

"Africa is nice."

The teeming wilderness, the bush, the animals, the jungle cats. God knows what goes on in Africa, must be a great place, a heathen place, hot. Virile. She tickles his sack. The place is full of life. Green, green. Yellow grass. Hot pink skies. The bed is burning. And his eyes are dilating further. This woman is a lion. He has never been to Africa. Or to many places in the southern hemisphere, for that matter. The bed is hotter than the Serengeti—wildlife is sprouting, children are shouting, lions are roaring—the wildlife of Africa is at his fingertips, her hair tangled, and it seems for just a second, home, this exotic climate. This is as close as he will get. This moment, before it all slips away.

A coy itching on his back springs his attention. He squirms to itch it and she laughs, down in the brush, hunting.

Bringing back the arch to her hips, the glow from the hallway light lights up her lower torso, its two little dimples, its full moon, a Goddess. He tickles her ear; she has on earrings he has not seen. Jess mounts him and just before melting, he thinks he is sleeping in a stranger's bed, one who is working his undeniable black magick from where nothing comes. He wants to find an herb that makes him potent in bed, rather than in mind. Pins and needles and he will soon be fast asleep, under the nuances of the other parents, Lillian's biological parents, the ones he wanted to be. He cannot wrap his head around the thought, who were they? But maybe it would come tomorrow, what he is looking for—life, truth—maybe it would come sometime in the night, like a visit from a stork, or a spirit. Maybe it would come to him. The one truth, though, reigns clear to him, the truth being: he has fathered this lie.

The lurid darkness is disturbed by a knock, not metallic nor wooden, but of glass. A snarl, raising the hairs on his arms and neck, is heard, followed by the star struck vibration of purring. He is seeing through his closed eyelids.

The Knock! Knock! of the moment is halted by the citrine and amethyst glare of a jungle beast—a lion—who is staring back at him, with the innate intellect of felines. The beast is power. He is helpless, he notices, just before taking a knee, naked. The jungle cat snarls and shows for a glimpse his teeth.

The vision opens to a boundless expanse, an interior notion of gargantuan borders, his knees brushing against the fronds and savannah grass and sound—the locusts, thousands of them—flying upwards into the cirro-stratus clouds, the crest of consciousness, of Africa. The wind takes his attention to the west, where the ball of incredulous fire flames, the sun warming his skin and emblazoning the beast's eyes, the warmth inviting the pilot into the bosom of mother Africa. He is here.

The lion strafes across his periphery. His phantasmagoric coat and iridescent eyes anchor him, keeping him from soaring toward the light. And he turns south toward the lion and hears again the Knock! Knock! which seems to be coming from the top of his skull, this knocking, the choking fallacy of tears, heat, sun, and sparks. His mind is riveted, ever-changed in this infinite moment. "Wake up," calls the knock, blurred by a higher frequency. The dichotomy of earth and air are finding each other. And the words, "Wake up," the knocks, the tears, the omni-flowing shards and jewels pouring now from the beast's glare, push Davis Parker toward nostalgia; he is out of step, not meant to witness the regal matter of this place. "Wake up!" He turns, and somewhere in the non-space between he and the distant tree line is a forsaken pane of glass. And the knocking calls—"Wake up! Wake up!"—heard by him, his lasting recognition of this lion.

Planes. That is what they are. He is looking through the planes, looking through the window onto the landscape below, the planes that take him from place to place, which blast the light back off him and into the eye of the sun; he has been kissed.

His vision dims to a gray darkness, this place never to be seen again.

His vision returns, the Sun, draping him in the barcode that never fails to present itself. Jess is awake; she is not in bed, and he can smell again the Kenyan brew downstairs. A quick puree and what was once a bean is now powder. Try grinding beans with your own hands. Impossible! Nevertheless, the smell calls and he is downstairs, his arms around his wife, Lillian playing on her handheld.

"I had a crazy dream last night, dad," she says.

"A crazy dream?" Davis replies. "A crazy dream. What happened?"

"I was swimming in water and there were fish all around me."

Davis pats her head, walks to the coffee machine, and then pours himself a cup of Kenyan coffee.

It is the day before his next trip. He will fly out to New York and boast the seven hour commute to nowhere as he lands with grace on the tarmac. But today, the Osbergs are over for dinner. Jess has been working, preparing sauce and potatoes, while Davis is outside grilling the Mahi Mahi. The smoke rises into his eyes.

Thirty years he has been flying these planes, along the pathways of the gods and still cooking right here in this spot is his favorite place in the world. This grill, the same old smoke, the same old tears, sweat, and salivation. He sips his beer. Fruity, the ale smacks his lips and he loves it, the air, the frothy bubbles, the buzz. It just keeps going. The fun never stops. It just keeps rolling and rolling, like wheels on a hill with kids inside them. Lillian is in the pool with her floaties, trying to see if she can hold her breath for more than thirty seconds, looking for fish.

The Osbergs will be coming in about thirty minutes from now, them and their two kids, along with their casserole, which Charlie Osberg has leaked to Davis is incredible. Charlie has also confided he is trying to keep everything under his belt, working out of London now, a little too far from the sunshine down here in the South, but it does well for him, he says. A little rain never hurt anyone.

The doorbell rings and Jess answers it in her canary yellow sundress, the same she wears every Saturday evening when they have people over. It is like a tradition. It gives her this glow she likes, and the house mirrors it back. It is a good ultimatum. It makes the visitors feel just right.

She answers with her normal cheer, "Hey, Charlie, Beth, welcome! Come in!" And the date is off—the cheery noise, the kids laughing and screaming, the men huddle after minutes outside, polishing off another one of those cold ones, the ladies swirling their dresses, the sun bright and the sky blue and ivory.

"It's much too great, being back in the state of Florida," says Charlie. "I miss it."

"Gets me every time," says Davis. "Every time I come back, it gets me, how healthy the air is. It seems full of vitamins, minerals, somehow."

Charlie's two boys are chasing Lillian. She has cooties, they say. They are trying to cure her. The Mahi Mahi is begging to be eaten. The potatoes are bursting. And underneath it all, the bellies are being thrummed with the anticipation of another child, Beth's third. "We're not sure what we're going to name it. In fact, we're going to wait to see the gender."

"Indeed," says Davis, glad for his friend.

The kids are out, tired, watching T.V. for the last hour before the Osbergs head home, back to the hotel. "It's Disney tomorrow," says Charlie. "The kids have never been."

"Likewise, neither has Lil." With a farewell kiss, the party disperses. The morning comes, the sun is blistering, the birds are chirping, and eyes are wide.

Something has happened, though.

Davis Parker is walking down the jet way, checks his

watch, and sees he is right on time. The plane will leave on schedule and they will be in New York for dinner. But something is missing. Between the drive out here, security, thinking about last night's meal—the boys, the Osbergs—he notices that the flame is gone. He knows what he needs. He needs the sky.

Luminescence blots out his vision of the world, the dials and switches, the gauges and frequencies. He sees now his life. As they taxi out, out toward where the ground ends and the air begins, he feels electricity, a twinge in his belly, the controls in his palms, the headset over his ears. He hears the words, "You are clear for take off." And he pushes the throttle. One-hundred-and-five tons of steel and cargo gets pushed by the Rolls Royce engines off the ground, at an incline of thirty degrees. He sees the clear image: the blue sky, crowning in through the windshield. It has hit; this is life. A blue sky limitless in the horizon, a child to raise and make one's own, a clue in life, where it is going, where to turn.

Far down, people are tiny, buildings are bricks, cars are toys. They fall away, too far below to be seen. The incline is too high, the angle too small. He needs to find a way, he thinks, a way to capture this feeling, like a firefly in a jar. Because that is what life is like, a firefly, and we are all just seeing it along, watching it live out its life. Everything he has known is in one glass case, delicate snow falling over the houses below. He is nearing New York. Through the windows, into the blue expanse through which he is flying, he captures a person, a long-faced, a bonafide revolutionary. He descends and lands the plane on the ground. His feet are anchored and he breathes in the cold air of New York. Flurries turn to a heavy snowfall. He is in the north again, but feels home more than ever, a wandering, lustful person, finding everything he has needed—a stratum that is never-ending, one ample and his to nurture.

For I Was Lost

For this son of mine was dead and has come to life again; he was lost and has been found. And they began to celebrate.
Luke 15:44

Two brothers walked along the shore, north of Celeste Point, watching the meteor shower. Keeping them apart yet together was the air, the innocuous splendor of good tidings and serenity between them. It was very gracious, the way the water surged upon the shore, breathing in unison with the brothers, who gazed through the stratosphere, glanced oblique at a meteor traveling through Sagittarius.

"It's a mystery," said the eldest, a man not young in the face, poised beside the younger, a full beard, wide-set eyes, blue and transfixing, seductive, alabaster skin, brown, dry hair, an impervious gait, and sunken temples, hair shoulder length and reminiscent of oak forests, gallant, treasured by the younger a true hero. The role model having raised the younger from the age of thirteen still held an untold wonder toward the boy, the younger, who was aged now twenty years and who had an improvised, jocular demeanor. "It's such a mystery, the Universe."

The younger said: "Indeed, it is."

The eldest stated: "It is as if there is a plan, you know, for everything."

The younger hummed is assent, an agreement between them, a transposed unity binding the inseparable brothers through time and space, the love, the compassion, the kindness having wrought through Fate's genius passion resplendence and worthiness. They walked along in the descending color of the evening, a darkening hue of indigo mixed in with the innate yellowness that seemed to emanate from the farthest reaches of nighttime, illuminating the sand before them, like the lunar surface and the Earthen ground, juxtaposed and agreeing to taste the opposite, hitting a mark. Another three meteors raced through the dark sky. They watched, awed at the cosmos's grandeur, a true coming through of ethos, Earthy and celestial. "When should we head back?" The younger brother sifted through the sand, barefooted. In his hand were his two sandals. He kicked the sand. He toyed with the notion that his elder brother's psyche was skewed, the elder seeing in items too much, seeing in items illumined meanings, symbols that God existed, symbols that their parents had passed with honor and dignity. That was twenty years prior this night. The brothers had found a certain coyness in the world.

Across the grassy lots atop of which had perched homes of a varying size and shape and across the railroad tracks was their grandparents' home, with whom they had lived over the past five years since their parents passed, tragic and sudden; whereas across the ocean shot here and there meteors, across the ocean resided people, countries, and women, wines, beers, and art of which the brothers would never see—for they had no intentions of leaving home—people and objects treasured by the world, but to both brothers small and unneeded. Art, as the eldest saw it, was in the ocean, in the sky, in his brother even, in the small exchanges between nature and the human, between the human and the human. Humidity clung to the brothers' arms and on the napes of their neck. They were to return home presently, but not before dipping their feet into the ocean for a nice salt bath. Once upon the shore again and across the sand, back to the pavilion where they had left their truck, they were to wash their feet in the cool, fresh water of the shower. It was always a pleasant way to finish off a trip to the beach; and both brothers as they meandered into the water held up their pants, lifting the hems of their khakis so as not to wet them and each of them enjoyed the water, the night, and the company, which was as the stars tended to acknowledge limited in terms of time.

"I," said the youngest, "am ready to go."

"Same," said the elder brother, and they both traversed the plane of sand to the pavilion, where they rinsed off their feet and then entered their truck.

"Thanks for coming with me." The trip to the beach for the meteor shower had been the eldest brother's idea and, coming to terms with some innate conflict in the boy (his brother who was at times standoffish and proud) the eldest smiled and turned the ignition, starting the truck and their voyage back to the home within which was sleeping Grandpa John and Grandma Irene. Both brothers loved their grandparents very much and in seeing them for meals at their kitchen table of stew or meat, boiled potatoes or crawfish, gave both brothers a gay and high sense of self. They saw in themselves their grandparents, like superimposed images of a tertiary consciousness, a conscience or a protector. The dichotomy of living in that house, the creaky floorboards, the peeling wallpaper, the shabby and tin roof, combining itself with a lofty understanding of the circumstances, kindness, truth, and adoration, rendered the brothers conscious but limited awareness that life and its joys were scarce. That was the impression given living in that home. Thankfulness, gratefulness. As the brothers pulled up into the gravel drive of that house, they, separate but conjoined at the crown, thought of the Heavens, their parents, and the meteor shower that proved the two existed and were related and harmonious.

The most lavish part of the house was the front patio, adorned with pine trees placed, it seemed, by some sort of omniscient hand here and there, a grouping of desert roses, saw grass just off the property line. Two seats, the kind one folds up after use, sat immovable in that patio—the brothers never moved them but sat in those thrones daily, scouring the property for flaws, which could be repaired, and fallacies, over which could be philosophized. The eldest, having been influenced by Grandpa John in recent years, had begun smoking cigarettes. An ashtray, filled with ashes and butts, sat on an end table between the seats ready for the morning's convening smoke. Convalescent, the smoke every morning cleared the mind of the eldest—he had dreams, strange and arcane, since his parents had passed—and smoking in the morning, he claimed, helped in vanquishing lingering daemons. It did seem that in that room, a room the brothers shared for sleep, there was an omnipresent lurking in the corners of phantoms and mocking, transparent beasts, which sought not to comfort the eldest but beckon him into a world of escape and volition. He, however, remained faithful to his grandparents and to morality, while his brother who snored opposite him on the southern wall had to be many times pulled from cliques and places that were detrimental—dealers' and whore houses and gang spots. The past year had been one of healing for the youngest. He had not gone back with that filth, the eldest thought to himself, to be molested by vagary. All he needed was his family and faith and, to a degree, luck, which would take him out of, remove him from this impoverished place in which they lived. Their parents were not wealthy; nor were their grandparents; and as time came to pass this fact settled level on the shoulders of the youngest, who wanted to escape the unreliable reality in which they lived, find wealth, and escape this hindered environment. It was a dream, a day-dream, which held him stagnant, as the eldest worked as a mechanic, the dream that one day he would escape and enter a world of possibilities, of riches and of congeniality. Of late, he had internalized his philosophy on the subject was incorrect, that an education was the way out, the first step to betterment and empowerment, wealth and abundance, not flight.

They slept, now, as the night turned to day. Rising above the sympathetic pines was the tribunal sun. The morning creaked into liveliness. Grandpa John was up and was making his way outside for a cigarette. He had his own chair, off to the left of the brothers'. He would sit and puff with a cup of coffee on his own end table and read the morning paper, sip more coffee and smoke another cigarette. He, ordinary and simple, was retired from the army, had fought in World War II and in the Korean War, and had seen his share of bloodshed and death. He asked now for only silence and peace, a harmonious resurgence of the morning with night, a cigarette at dawn when the sparrows chirped and dipped through the pines and when the crickets, likewise, chirped still in the heady morning way of things, procuring dreams for the slumberous.

The eldest boy woke at a snap in the floorboards, the house settling. He rose and stepped into his khakis, put on a light undershirt, and moved outdoors.

"Ah, John, come, have a seat with me."

John was his father's name. It had been a tradition to name the eldest son after the father; thus, so was named John the grandfather. John lit up a cigarette and sat in his seat. The morning was cool still and exhaled the beginning of a young day. The day was going to stay cool, at a modest sixty or seventy degrees, it being winter, the month of December.

"How did you sleep?" asked Grandpa John.

"Same," said John. "Same. Dreams, dreams."

"I know it," said the grandfather. "It could be good luck."

"Not these dreams," said John. "There's a lot of darkness, a profound and endless black I go into. There's no way out. It's not good luck, Grandpa, not at all."

Grandpa John stayed quiet. He took a drag off of his cigarette. He said, "Get something out of them? You know, a lot of smart, smart people say there's something about dreams, something that makes you understand, something that makes you human."

"Human, beast, what's the difference? What's the difference when you're getting attacked?"

"Reason."

"There's no reason," said John, "it's all a bunch of malarkey, bull. If it meant something, I'd know it."

"There's nothing interesting in the paper today, John."

"That I do know. There never is. They feed you bull."

"People love bull."

"People love bull," John agreed. "Say, I'll go in and make us breakfast."

"Sounds good," said Grandpa John.

"How do you want your eggs?"

"Make them over-easy, thank you. Over-easy'll do."

John walked in through the front door. He had finished his cigarette halfway. He had snubbed it out before it was done. Talking about dreams frustrated him. His heart raced sometimes in his dream; and just when it seemed he was arriving somewhere, he woke with a start, cut short of the end. It frustrated him.

In the kitchen, Grandma Irene was pouring herself a cup of coffee. "Good morning," she said. Feeble, she had aged much since John's original recollection of her.

"Good morning, Grandma." He took four eggs from the refrigerator. "Would you like some eggs, Grandma?"

She said, "No, I'll have my toast."

"Toast it is," said John. He put a thin slice of butter on the skillet which was on the burner and waited for it to melt. When it did, he tilted the skillet on all ends to spread around the butter. Then, he cracked two eggs into the skillet. The eggs bubbled and heaved, thickened and whitened. He flipped over the eggs, let them cook for five seconds more, and put them on a plate. He repeated the procedure. Presently, two eggs lay on either plate. John went outside to retrieve Grandpa John. He was having another cigarette, exhaling smoke, meditative. The morning had become a warm orange. "Eggs are ready, Grandpa," John said.

"I'll be in in a second," Grandpa John said. "Don't wait for me, start eating."

John returned to the table. He picked up his fork and started eating. John dipped a piece of bread into the yolk. He did so as Grandpa John walked in. Grandpa John sat down and began eating his eggs. He smelled of smoke. In the living room, the television had started. Grandma Irene would be watching Good Morning America. On this day everything seemed well. On this day everything seemed good. The blue tinge of television light trickled into the kitchen through the open door and John thought what a curious invention the television was. That was what he needed to do: invent something, something grand, something curious, something everybody needed—he did not know where to start—an invention that changed the way people lived, an invention that changed the way people drove cars, washed their clothes, put their babies to sleep, washed dishes, brushed their teeth, shampooed their hair. He needed to invent something that changed the way people made love, asked questions, worked, prayed, and ate. It had to be an invention of momentous effect, an invention that changed the human. The television thrummed. Grandma Irene laughed.

"I'm going outside," said Grandpa John.

"I'll join you," said John.

They stepped outside into the winter day and noticed two squirrels. The squirrels were chasing each other. There was a cycle living here on Trolley Court, a cycle that was reluctant to be broken. Trolley Court had been John's home for many years. He wanted to grow up, leave Trolley, and live on his own. He did not mind if his brother stayed with him—if he found a job they might even be able to do it—but working at the mechanic's part time and making a minimal income, John could not justify living on his own just yet. He lit up a cigarette as his brother walked outside.

"Jim," said Grandpa John. "Good morning!"

"Morning, Grandpa John."

"How did you sleep?"

"Like a lamb."

"Good, good."

Jim sat in his chair. He looked up through the pines. He said, "It's fixing to be a good day today."

"Indeed, it is," said Grandpa John.

"I was thinking about going into town and looking for a job," Jim said.

John was impressed. "That sounds like a good idea."

"Would you want to go in with me, John?"

"I think," John said, honest, "it would be best if you go in yourself. They want to see independence, you know."

"I know it," said Jim.

John took a drag from his cigarette. John knew Jim despised tobacco. He had started letting him off, though. Jim was not racking John so much anymore about smoking. "Do we need anything from the store, Grandpa?"

"I don't need anything," said Grandpa John. "Ask Grandma."

"I'll ask her," said Jim, and he went inside.

John continued puffing on his cigarette. He watched Grandpa John with intensity. Grandpa John started coughing. He spat black.

"It's best if you quit these things," Grandpa John said.

"I know it," said John, and he snubbed out his cigarette. He had to go into work. He, after a shower, was going to leave and would arrive in just about an hour's time. It was going to be as his brother said, a nice but a long day.

Jim sat with his head leaned back. He sat on a recliner, not listening to the television, which shimmered incessant before him; floral wallpaper, torn upholstery, chipped and worn tables, stained lamp shades, dated trinkets, a deer's rack, a painted river scene, shredded paperback books, a carpet tower in which the cat meditated, the cat, his grandmother's purring at the five o'clock news—all these itemized representations of intellectual repression rendered Jim into a state of trance, the blue hue and the blackness behind his eyelids mitigating. He remembered his parents. They were young when they passed. Thirty-three. He could remember the services with lucidity. Purple cushions, pews, crying strangers. A priest. The church bells. It filled him with nostalgia, a tepid water filled his sinuses, daring him not to cry. The recollection splashed cunning into his eyes. He opened them. Turning toward his grandmother, he reconnoitered the level field through which they communicated, a turning, tumultuous scape of understanding, forgiveness, laughter, remembrances, and said, "Grandma, how long have you been married?"

"Oh, Jim, I've forgotten. I stopped counting, oh, five, ten years ago. It must be thirty years, now. Yes, Grandpa John and I have been married thirty years. Oh, how time flies. How time flies."

Jim closed his eyes, sorry he had asked. It seemed to fill Grandma Irene with an objectiveness not far from patronizing. She saw in him wisdom, she relayed, one fervent evening when Grandpa John was not himself. He had been coughing up blood again. "You must get him to a doctor," Jim had said.

"Oh," Grandma Irene had said. "You are wise."

They never took him to a doctor. He coughed up blood. He just coughed and coughed. It was becoming in the errant, chain-smoking lifestyle a kind of superfluous presence, the coughing, a presence that Grandpa John refused to acknowledge or fear or revere. He, after the wars in which he fought, feared nothing. Death was a time, a change, a shifting of spirit which Grandpa John considered in the coyest of terms "Proper." It was, in his way of thinking, a man's duty to live and die and fertilize the Earth, giving back to that unrefined mass. He did not believe in God. Many times he had extrapolated the fact that when life took a turn toward the realest mode, such as in war or in sickness, fear was not an attribute, an aspect that the world took to with kindness. It was stagnation, fear, like taking a teaspoon of molasses and hoping for the best. Hope, for that matter, was not in Grandpa John ready vocabulary. He was a man that believed in Fate. He was a man that believed in vigor. Grandpa John, in his psychology, was the healthiest man Jim had ever met.

Grandma Irene, from somewhere in the ether said, "Jim Harold Joseph, are you hungry?"

He had, in fact, grown hungry. He had not eaten anything since breakfast. "I could eat," he said.

A splendid night overcame the house on Trolley Court with calm reserve, which sunk mystified into the cool sands on which the house was situated. John had come home from work and was enjoying a beer and a cigarette on the patio with his brother, who, as the sun set and as the shades of green foliage became blue then black and as the sky transformed into an opalescent mine shaft full of diamonds shimmering, sipped, too, a beer and hummed into the chromatic spectral lights of the atmosphere, hummed along with the sparrows who dived and chirped, resplendent in their midst; for it was on this night, Jim's birthday, that a present in the form of a metallic automobile was given to the younger brother upon John's arrival back home.

The silver Chevrolet Impala was not lavish to any extent; it was famished of all hydration, a pure beater in all regards, but to the younger brother's liking, tinted in the windows, which were power controlled, and with greased rims, which shone incandescent in the twilight from the Joseph's dirt drive. He had entered the car with a woebegone interest, looking at the innards of the Chevy with fervent apprehension, wanting to take it for a drive. The car ran well—not a tick in the engine, not a squeak in the shocks—and Jim, opulent and in control, pulled back into the dirt drive where Grandpa John had been waiting following their short spin around the neighborhood.

"Drives great," he said. Talking about the car gave him a shrill chill down his spine, like something dormant in his ego had been unlocked and given full regard. Nothing so lavish as of yet had been granted him, a car, the concern, the good-nature of his brother, John, who had kept this a secret, not even having told Grandpa John or Grandma Irene. It was an awakening for Jim. He had lived in cordial compliance within that house on Trolley Court, and now he had wheels, freedom to exit the neighborhood and roam—where? Nashville? New York?—anywhere he wished. Dirt already caked the sides of the silver car and the chrome rims. Jim did not mind. He was taken up in the thermal of hot air and an expectation of dinner, which awaited him. Fried tilapia and asparagus. It was coming into form, his futuristic and enamored spirit, and unlike his brother he foresaw trips to the Florida-Georgia border to pick up 40 oz. beers of cheap malt liquor. John would of course accompany him. Tomorrow was Sunday.

Jim asked over dinner, "John, do you want to go to Georgia tomorrow?"

"What for?" He poked his tilapia, cut another piece, and deposited the fish into his mouth, and then he took a sip of beer.

"Why not? For fun? I want to get some stuff at the Florida-Georgia border."

John, chewing, took a second to get his food down.

When he did, he said, "Sure."

The following day, four hours northward, Jim and John Joseph, driving on Interstate 95, in placated rhythm, tended toward their destination—a small town on the border of Florida-Georgia known as Jacksonville. Jim, driving, weaved in and out of cars, having picked up the speed of the christened Chevrolet to a haughty eighty-five miles per hour. They had with them a flask of Jim Beam and a six pack of Coca-Cola. Jim said, "So, how did you end up with this car, anyway? How did you afford it?"

John, morose, looked at Jim and afforded the comment, "I have my ways."

"But, how?" said Jim.

"You really want to know?"

"Yes," Jim said, "I really want to know. How did you afford this car?"

"The truth is," John said, "I didn't afford it. There's no way I could afford it. It was given to the shop, as a junker."

"A junker, huh?"

"A junker, and I fixed it up on my own time."

Having returned home, the chorus of gravel, the twisting of the tires on the dirt drive, the breeze through the sawgrass granting them a welcome entrance, the two brothers walked tangent to one another up the drive and into the home, which was silent save the humming of the air conditioning unit, thrummed like a bicycle with a playing card in its spokes.

The trip up to Jacksonville and a small town just over the border of Georgia proved fruitful and generous, the two brothers having picked up a case of beer, the two brothers having conversed on issues such as pollution in the Gulf, reincarnation, Appalachia, World Trade One, the history of Persia, the inquisition, how Catholicism and organized religion was the beginning of the end, Revelations, equestrianism, Pigmy Indians. A wealth of knowledge found in the other, brazen and pure, lent arbitrary sparks of intellect in cephalon-caudal locales, intellect, inspiration, spirituality reaching an apex, a white summit, where the brothers found residence, fire, warmth, a transmuted fixation on the other, their origins, their centers of quality, the numerous and well-filled, centric tendencies, which tended toward the completeness found in the other; for each of them saw in the other themselves, an idyllic reflection, which resounded and echoed the rudiments of joy back to the forefront of conversation from the recesses of movement and identity. John had just had a cigarette before saying, "Jim, I'm going to bed. I am exhausted."

"Good night, John." Jim, hungry, would stay up for a midnight snack, a second dinner of cold cuts—cheese, ham, and mayonnaise between two pieces of whole wheat bread. The night was wondrous, the trip up the coast, which brought them to the beaches of Jacksonville and a rather charming stretch of Route 1. The beach, azure and clear, was a fixed notion to the younger of the brothers, a notion or exclamatory point that life, dark matter, a silver lining wrapped him in a certain tissue that seemed not too far removed from divine. Unordinary, he had spoken out on the thought: "It's so vast," thinking if his parents through an auditory phenomenon in cosmology were listening, hearing him, nodding and agreeing and embracing the sound waves of his voice, catching them in nets like Lepidoptera, to observe and let loose. Jim, in that locale, felt an undefined freedom which had been unfelt in all his years. Alone, in regards to his thoughts, he sent out a prayer out to the ocean, praying for peace. Grandma Irene came out of her bedroom in her night gown, floral and light. She had been sleeping.

"Jim, how was your drive?"

"It went well, Grandma," he said, finishing the cold cut sandwich in one last bite. "It's late," he said. "I'm going to bed."

"I don't blame you. Sleep well, Jim." She turned, waiting not for a response. Jim's eyes were good night enough for her; and she closed her door with a timid squeak. Jim got up and went to the refrigerator for a glass of water and drank it. It cooled him, his bones and his throat, the element with which he had identified hours ago.

He took off his shirt and shorts and climbed into bed, kept one foot suspended in midair so as to brush off the remaining sand, and then the other, and swung his feet into the cool pocket within which he fell asleep seconds later.

He woke in what seemed ten minutes. The morning was bright. He rose. Getting out of bed, it seemed as though a cool wind carried in his lungs lifted him and rejuvenated him after the long, black slumber, inviting him into the day. He went outside to where John was. He was still home. He was with Grandpa John, smoking a cigarette.

He said, "Work called me. I'm off today. What shall we do?"

Jim, surprised and pleasant, said nothing, but smiled,

and then sat in his chair beside his brother, who still was looking at him with his own grin spread from ear to ear across his broad handsome face, taking a drag of the cigarette, blinking, looking at Jim, an endearing presence, possibilities, forthcomings, premonitions, the cigarette short, John snubbing it out, exhaling smoke from his nostrils, and then saying: "Huh?"

Jim: "Oh, I don't know. I'm sort of beached out."

"I know it. Me, too," said John.

Grandpa John: "How was your guys' trip to north Florida and Georgia?"

Jim: "It was swell, Grandpa, swell."

John: "I think we'll just drink beer all day."

Jim: "That sounds like a plan," and that was what they did all day, on the day following their trip to Georgia.

The day scintillating, the night feigning, the brothers foolhardy, entered the late stages of night, drunken on Georgian malt liquor and talking of girls and money. The sun, rising golden in four hours still lingered in the hindquarters of the Earth, in Cambodia and Australia, the same time John and Jim Joseph were drinking to the agreeable climate, the clarified epithelial squamous of starlight, their cotton backdrop dyed indigo. Innate youthfulness had been revived in the night, the North star shimmering in harmony with Ursa Minor, Levanah peering through the pine trees and coloring to fancy the patio, the front lawn purple, a hitherto unnamable source of circulating energy, mysterious and clinging like unrefined apes to the backs of their parents, a cloud, dark and foretelling, the future, the cosmos, climaxing and epitomizing.

John spoke, “I can’t breathe.” He had been laughing. Jim, attempting to burn a dried leaf from the nearby azalea, drunk, missed the leaf with the light and had made contact with the flame, with the tip of his finger. “You numbskull.”

“Hey, watch it, bozo. If you only knew the amount of style housed in that finger.” They, harmonious, took a sip of beer. “No big deal.”

Akin to the sleight of hand, managed by his younger brother, John had lit a cigarette, an extended part of himself, a breath full of wit, mercy from the ensuing hilarity, damning and conclusive. “After this cigarette, I’m going to sleep. I’m tired and drunk.”

“You are drunk,” said the younger brother. “Drunkard.”

“Speak for yourself. I’m not the one who got upended at Marty’s for running his mouth.”

“That was New Year’s Eve and I was all sorts of stoned.”

“Nevertheless, what’s fact is fact.”

“What’s fact is fact, but I didn’t see you come running to help.”

“I was with that girl, what was her name? who later got pregnant?”

“I forget.”

“Probably for the best.”

“Definitely for the best.”

John finished his cigarette and snubbed it out in the ashtray. He, rising in five hours, for work, needed the sleep. Jim, reconnected with his good-nature, agreed, stepped indoors with his brother. They went to sleep, and they both were quite happy.

At the time the news reached John at work, Grandma Irene had already called the hospital. Jim, transfixed by the severity of the moment, had driven his new car to the mechanic's, where John worked, and had told him Grandpa John had had a stroke. He was no longer able to talk, to speak with clarity, the left side of his face, the Broca and Wernicke areas paralyzed and numb. The news came to John as a sudden wave of nausea, a surging of thick, diluted clouds, commingling with his frontal cortex and rendering him infused with vertigo. He had taken off from work, his last three hours of the work day at hand, and had put his bicycle in the car, and had been driven back to the house on Trolley Court just in time to see the ambulance, shiny and bright, round a corner out of sight, Grandpa John and Grandma Irene aboard; and a high sense of angst filled him, a tenebrous and pitchy frequency, thin and parallel, encompassing him. John, powerless, turned to Jim, who was parking the car in the dirt drive, and said, "What happened? How did you find him?"

Jim said, "We were on the patio. He was smoking a cigarette, like he always is, and I looked at him and he was fine, and I turned away, and I looked back, and his head was lolled to the side, and he was foaming at the mouth, real bad. It was going down his chin. I went inside, immediately, and got Grandma and called 911."

Perplexed, John exited the car, keeping his head low as he entered the house, took off his shoes, and went back outside. He lit up a cigarette and Jim sat with him in a manner so light that the factual evidence of the scene, Grandpa John's lit cigarette on the ground, seemed less cumbersome. John took a drag of his own cigarette. He picked up Grandpa John's and snubbed it out in the ashtray.

"Can I get you anything," asked Jim.

"A glass of water," said John.

"A glass of water," said Jim. "Are you hungry?"

"I couldn't eat now." The brothers, unlike other natural phenomena, operated on the level of understanding, which, unheard and unspoken, was communicable via a frequency of unrefined brotherliness; the boys knew each other's pain; their hardships were a conjoined conflict, like sandpaper on wood, the eldest being the championing symbol of perseverance, but this time the youngest took that role.

Jim, in the kitchen, felt an empowerment in his loins, a certain cue that rendered him, his brother, and the scenario a manageable pursuit, a fluid pursuit, which was able to seep through the fissures of reality like melting ice and which held the unexplored reaches of brotherhood. Jim carried a glass of ice water out through the front door and gave it to his brother, who accepted. He drank deep of the fluid, rejuvenating any otherwise parched or singed centers. He said, "Grandma is with Grandpa?"

"She is," was the reply, a meek sound having escaped from his brother's lips. It was rather unrepresentative to the way, in fact, Jim felt; and something was lost in the translative moment, a wisp of air taken up by the vacuum above Earth, the stratosphere, the aerial ecosystem that encompassed Trolley Court, Celeste Point, the beach, the entire planet, shaken and torn. Emanating through that blackness, through that vacuum was a certain light unseen by John, Jim, or Grandma Irene, a psychometric anomaly, pure, unrefined, and pragmatic. John finished his cigarette. Jim sat in the chair beside his brother. It was all very perfect, the way the moment glistened in the blue irises of the eldest; John began to cry. He knew not why. A sudden and resplendent fear was lifted from his shoulders as if something he had always known had been confirmed, obscure but crystalline, a dusty diamond, a node in the crown. His ears felt cold, the breeze, the emerald cloying of life, burlesque and confining. Release.

It was five-thirty and John knew Grandma Irene would stay in the hospital with Grandpa John. He rose, went inside, and changed into more comfortable clothing. Denim, a yellow button down. He felt he needed to possess a morsel of dignity. Thus, he rolled up his sleeves, went outside to ask his brother if he wanted to go for a walk down Trolley Court, visit the park near the main road, which went all the way to the beach. Jim suggested they take the car to the hospital. John laughed, admitted he was flustered. Entering the car, John already knew by some form of telegraphy that the news was not positive.

John and Jim Joseph walked into the hospital within a bubble of transmitted worry, noncommittal and deprecating. Sterilized walls, linoleum flooring. They asked the front office secretary in which room John Joseph was being kept. "Room 303," was the response, and the two brothers walked, coherent and alert, through the white halls to the elevator, which opened when John pushed the button.

Entrance had been granted to these two, to a higher state, a state of sensitive identification—mortality.

Upon entering Room 303, Jim and John were granted a glimpse of a pallid-skinned man and a weeping Grandma Irene, who was grasping Grandpa John's hand in hers, weeping and weeping, turning her head, her two boys in her vision, both tall, handsome, broad-shouldered, young, and virile, and said, "He's gone," shaking her head, her blue eyes bloodshot, negative colors, endearing, hopeful yet sad and bequeathed these two brothers.

Jim said, "I'm sorry. He's in a better place. He must be."

"He is," John said, and took his grandmother's hand. It was icy cold, sweaty. He knew not how to expound on that, that mere statement: "He's in a better place," death too much to think of, too direct, too perfect; a symmetric split between Grandpa John's liveliness and his dying disconnected a certain seam in John. He began to weep, torn amidst anxious hues of darkness and light, prodigal tears flowing from his eyes; grasping his grandmother's hands, he noticed his hands were callused. There was dirt and grime, oil under his fingernails. He was imperfect, a sordid amalgam of precise good and blurred bad, encumbered and physical. Grandpa John, now, was spiritual, a memory, his body lying as a empty shell, which housed his ideas, his beliefs, voided of a mind, which evaporated into the sheer beauty of death, Jim walking over, Jim putting his arm around his brother, breathing, alive, and likewise imperfect, a body, a material being with beige skin and white crescents on his fingernails and pink lips, Jim having succumbed to primordial ways of thinking—"Goodness gracious," he said—embracing his family, accosted not by smoke or substance, sober.

They stayed with the body for many minutes. A doctor, a white lab coat and stethoscope, who had pronounced Grandpa John dead, walked in with the morgue people. The transferred him to a rolling gurney. The doctor expressed condolences. The morgue people nodded their heads as they rolled out Grandpa John, still. John, Jim, and Grandma Irene were told they could go. There was nothing left to do. The silver Chevy downstairs fitted all three of them. John, Jim, and Grandma Irene went home, an emptier home. The grass out front still showed green; the pines still showered down every so often pine needles. Pine needles were scattered all around the front lawn. Nobody ever cleaned them up. The sky was topaz, a clear white and blue amalgamation, a window, transformative. Grandma Irene cooked eggs on the stove for dinner. She was very quiet. After cooking the eggs and eating, she went into the living room but did not turn on the television. She sat with one of the paperback books from the table that was pushed up against the wall. She read until morning.

Morning came; a gorgeous pink sky was cast from the East. "Behold," said John to Jim, who was outside with him, while John, smoking a cigarette, held fast the explicit nuances of the morning, calm, galvanized, an epitomized recalling of the previous night's dreams conjured in the eyes of the brother, beheld.

"It looks nice," said Jim. He had been drinking a glass of milk. A thin line of whiteness clung to the hair on his upper lip. "You're going to work in about an hour, I presume?"

"No," John said. "I called Phil and took off. He understands."

"Good." Grandma Irene came outside after an hour long sleep. "Good morning," Jim said.

"Good morning. I couldn't sleep, Jim, I tell you. I couldn't sleep." She choked up. "I could stop thinking of John."

"He was good to us all."

"He was a good man," she said, and went inside.

John was going to go through Grandpa John's side of the closet today. There was so much in that closet, World War II and Korean War memorabilia, Elvis records, Muddy Waters and B.B. King records, a record player, eight-track cassettes, a cassette player, worn shirts, suits, jeans, ties, tennis balls, golf clubs. John rose, snubbed out his cigarette, and went inside for breakfast. Grandma Irene was already cooking over easy eggs on the skillet for the boys. Two slices of toast were in the toaster oven. John was hungry and sat at the wooden table, magazines under one of its legs, and waited for breakfast. Jim, too, walked inside, also hungry for breakfast. Jim always had his eggs with ketchup, a staple in his diet—the cooked eggs, the sweet ketchup, the salt and pepper, the runny yolk.

"I," said John, "am going through Grandpa John's things today."

"Good, tell me what you find," said Jim, dark circles under his eyes; he had not slept well.

Breakfast was eaten by the two boys and their grandmother, the morning heat rising into a temperate day, Trolley Court shimmering. John went into Grandpa John's room. He opened the door to the closet. He had emptied a hamper to put into it items he wanted to keep. Already he saw a few things. The golf clubs, a neon Coca-Cola sign. He opened a shoebox and found quite a few baseball cards and old coins. He cast it aside and opened another. Inside the second shoebox, John found war medals and ribbons in cases, evidence of World War II and the Korean War, Grandpa John's fighting in them. He looked at them. There was a purple heart and a bronze star amongst other metals. They were all shiny and clean. He dared not take them out of their cases. John put the ribbons and medals in the hamper. Beneath the shoebox within which he found the ribbons and medals, John saw an army uniform and further back in the corner a rifle. John picked up the green fatigues and looked them over. They seemed well and in order. He tucked them away in the hamper and went to the rifle. Picking it up, John noticed the rifle was heavier than it looked. It was loaded. John knew not where any ammunition would be and thought if the rifle worked at all. It was all quite evident. Grandpa John, having left them so much to discover, had not told them of his journeys through Europe and the Orient during the wars. He had left that up to their imagination. Yes, it was all quite evident to John. Grandpa John had been a hero.

Jim said, "What is life?"

"Depends on who you ask," said John.

"I mean, really, is it worth it?"

"What? Are you thinking of euthanizing? Is your suffering so bad?"

The two were sitting, convalescing, two days following Grandpa John's death. The ground of the patio, a cement block, was covered in beach sand. They had brought it with them after their trip to the shore that morning. Amidst the blue and black coolness of the winter morning, they saw ship liners and oil rigs on the horizon; and Jim was wondering if life was compromised. He said, "It's just that, it seems too simple. Grandpa John was here, now he's gone, just like that." He sipped a bottle of beer. "Is it too hard to believe that life is, maybe, hallucinated? That life can't be just a kink in the rope, so to speak?" He was getting drunk.

John said, "You're over thinking it. As far as I see it, there are three things that make the world go 'round: Politics, money, and religion. Belong to any of the three, and you're golden. Fall outside of the bounds of riches, promiscuity, or hypocrisy, you're one-of-a-kind, a prodigy."

"You mean it?" Jim asked.

"It's something I've always believed," and John left it at that. He took another sip of his beer, a remaining bottle from their trip up to the Florida-Georgia border. He said, "I can only imagine how Grandma is feeling."

"She's down," Jim said.

John said, "She's down, all right." All day they had been drinking beer. All day Grandma Irene had been in her room reading and looking at pictures, photo albums from the 1960s and 1970s, and swimming trophies she had won in the fifties. An insufficiency of air seemed to percolate throughout the house. Trolley was a zone of temporal determination. Everybody was philosophizing. Grandpa John's passing had not only been surprising, it had been inconvenient.

A galvanized Jim, drunk and hitting some primordial mark, said, "When it all boils down to it, this is Paradise." It seemed, in this time, that a juxtaposition had taken place, constellations now Earthy, Earth now ethereal, all dancing, all glimmering. The night would come, a night long sought for, a night within which violet waves of light, a sojourn, crossed the waves of light brought on by the sun. Presently, the brothers commented on the orb that had arisen. The Epicurean moon shone over the horizon.

One Saturday night, John and Jim Joseph with two girls, Ashley and Tammy Reinhardt, went to a small bar on the beach. The quaint bar was built from the bottom up of wood. Wooden stools, a wooden bar, wooden tables here and there, with plastic table cloths, which red and glossy. The bar beneath the foursome's forearms maintained a static common ground.

They had ordered one pitcher of cheap light beer. Already, it was finished. "It's good to finally see your girls again," said John. "After Grandpa dying it is necessary to live, to shed."

The two ladies and the two gentlemen had gone to high school together, a large public school, a little too inland, too inland to call it a quality and well-kept school; there were obtuse degrees of sex and violence. Ashley, blonde and coerced by her sister into coming tonight, said, "It's our pleasure," a slight twang, Floridian and country, in her voice that admitted a cuteness, a subtle fuzziness, a Cottontail rabbit, her tan navel exposed. John Joseph looked her up and down, his pupils black nebulas silhouetted against protruding blue irises. Ashley had an effect on the older brother, a whitewash pureness emanating through his loins, an amplified coaxing that rendered him incapacitated. He drank his beer and said, "You two haven't changed a bit," the heavens rotating, the constellations revolving around the eldest siblings, John and Ashley, centric and eventual.

Beer turned to vodka and whiskey, the ladies drinking the vodka and the men drinking the whiskey. They walked outside of the backdoor onto the beach. On the beach, a grouping of people were having a fire and music and dancing were heard and seen.

The day had diminished into an evening of foretold apogee, an apex of reasoning beckoning the two brothers out to the bar as well as the two sisters. They approached the fire. Orange and red, it cackled in the darkness, a well-construed, temporal entity the night conjured and convalesced. Beer, acoustic music, crescendo, the composite chatter of well over twenty people, the women dancing, the men speaking, dogs barking, having rendered the sisters and brothers into a state of reverie, mixed with the vibratory strings of their hearts; expectations like marionettes, Fate taking a hold, an evening of proportionate tidings, surging onto the shore. Cruise ships and oil rigs on the horizon, a yellow retriever bathing in the Atlantic Ocean. John pulled Ashley aside: "Would you like to go for a walk down the beach?" The answer was an precocious yes; and they walked northward toward the pier and a small pavilion, which was surrounded by saw grass and mangroves. Jim and Tammy Reinhardt stayed with the procession of people, who were drinking and dancing.

A little further up the beach, John, abashed and rather timid, pulled Ashley toward the pavilion. They sat, drank, and talked, and then there was a lull in the conversation. John pulled her and kissed her. She kissed him back with her tongue and then kissed the corner of his mouth and then his ear. It all happened very fast.

In memory of Grandpa John, John, Jim, and Grandma Irene decided to create a garden, and visited a nursery for plants. The three, jubilant, entered John's pickup truck and headed westward, a dirt road becoming paved, and then dirt again, John envisioning cherry blossoms, ligustrums, lemon trees, quite enraptured by the thought of it all, and then pulling into the nursery, one Saturday morning, the bed of the pickup truck cleaned out in order to transport the trees and plants back to Trolley Court. Scents of rose petals, soft and serene, and soil, rich and smart, was inhaled by the trio and emanated throughout the nursery, which was colorful, spectacular to the point that John and Jim were quite taken aback by the sight of it all, so much so that they went to the customer service desk and asked for assistance. Along with the brothers, Grandma Irene, delicate in her age, felt a subtle sense of reverie encompassing her, penetrating her aged bones, and making there an ambrosial subjectiveness.

"We are going to need some help," said John to a pretty lady, who had dirt caked onto her hands and who wore green overalls. "We're looking to create a garden in front of our house, with some nice bushes, flowers, maybe, and a tree."

The pretty lady, who was just then shifting fertilizer, turned and asked, "Will you be maintaining the plants on a regular basis?"

John said, "I would think so."

"Right this way," said the pretty lady, "and we'll get you guys settled with a good half dozen or so plants." Navigating through the miasmic floral life, the pretty lady, followed by John, Jim, and Grandma Irene, took the trio to the trees. "We'll look for some smaller foliage later," she said, "but, for now, we'll look for a good center piece to your garden," her absentmindedness rendering her, and the others who followed her in the element, an oblique sureness, a woebegone demeanor granting the pretty lady a contagious ambivalence. Sugar palms, cypresses, cherry blossoms. John sneezed. The pretty lady said, "I, for one, think a good fern in the center of your garden would be a good ultimatum, a sort of easy umbrella-like tree. It would lend good shade."

"What do you think about a fern?" asked John to Jim.

"I like that," Jim said.

"What do you think about a fern?" John asked Grandma Irene.

She said, "I think Grandpa would have loved it."

"I think we'll do the fern," said John.

"Very well," said the pretty lady. "I'm going to give you some lilacs and roses, too, that will fill in your garden nicely."

"Good," John said. "Very good," quite aware of his amateurish state.

"We'll ring you up at the counter and I'll get a few guys to put this tree and some mulch in the back of your pickup truck."

Departing the nursery, John took care in making turns, navigating back to Trolley Court. He and his brother, all day, were going to be digging and planting the trees and flowers. It was nearing ten o'clock A.M. and when they arrived back to the home on Trolley Court, the two brothers unloaded the pickup truck of the fern, the lilacs, the roses, and the mulch and set them down on the front lawn. First, the lawn was to be picked up and the grass was to be mowed. John sat in the appropriate chair and lit up a cigarette. As Jim mowed the lawn, John smoked and thought. He thought of the garden, he thought of Ashley Reinhardt, he thought of the beer he had in the refrigerator, he thought of Grandpa John, and all was metronomic, a ticking reverberating through him, keeping him affixed, meditative, thoughtful, and observant, a composer of sights, an artist who would create color in a place which was darkened by shadows and dreams and who was accosted by the sympatric notion of life and death. He finished his cigarette, all too aware it was indeed unhealthy and that he was shortening his life. Jim was finished mowing presently, John approached him with a shovel in hand, and they, harmonic, went to work on the garden.

Around three o'clock, the fern was planted in the front lawn, mulch was poured around the fern, and rain had begun falling, driving the brothers inside underneath the patio for water and another cigarette. "It looks good, honestly." John was admiring the work they had done. A cool bright green, the light, sensitive leaves of the fern, the dark red mulch, its thick scent—all comprised quite an atmosphere created by the two; and as if on cue, pulling up to the house on Trolley Court was a small Volkswagen. Out came Ashley Reinhardt to John's surprise. She walked up and through the new garden with an air of self-confidence and classiness, and then looked John square in his eyes as she stood on the patio in her white sun dress and sandals. "John, Jim, good afternoon."

"Good afternoon," said John. "Ashley! What a pleasant surprise. Can I get you a water or a beer?"

"No, thank you, John. I'm all right." She sat in Grandpa John's old chair. "Say, John, can I speak to you in private for a moment?"

The brothers exchanged glances. John said, "Sure, sure."

Jim got up and walked inside the house.

"I had a great time the other night," said John.

"I know," she said. "So did I. As a matter of fact, the reason why I'm here pertains to that night."

"Oh?"

"John," Ashley said. "I'm late."

"You're late? You mean you're pregnant?"

"I might be pregnant, John, and it can only be you."

John, grounded now, said, "And you're sure it's mine?"

"It can be nobody else," Ashley said. Her green eyes flickered, met his, and then dropped away. "I like what you're doing to the place," she said, talking of the garden.

"Thanks," he said. "We've been at it all day, and then

it started to rain." The rain had picked up to a steady shower, which was now soaking the ground. He said, "Are you going to have the baby?"

"If, in fact, I am pregnant, I would like to have the baby," she said, "yes."

"I'm not against it," he said, and that was truthful.

She said, "You will be a good father."

"Thanks," he said. "Thanks a lot. That's great. That's lovely."

When Jim came back outside, Ashley Reinhardt was gone. John did not say anything at first; he observed the parabolic circumvention, which predominated the home on Trolley Court, for there had been an exit and now there was going to be an entrance, a portentous, lighthearted manner in which the next nine months would preside. As if preconceiving this synchronicity, in that circumvention—Grandpa John's exit, John's child's entrance—Jim, dimensional, had said, "What was that all about?"

"Ashely Reinhardt," John said, "is pregnant. I'm the father."

Jim stayed quiet, letting disperse the density of those words, and then said, "That's great, isn't it?"

"It's great," said John. "It's great."

Tenebrous, Jim slapped John on the shoulder and then shook his hand. It was quite a time, the winter of that year for the Josephs, and as time unfolded further a certain quality seemed inescapable, a sureness in which John Joseph, Jim Joseph, Grandma Irene, and even Grandpa John from his ethereal and limitless height did not dismiss. It was too prevalent, too considerable, a linear extension of life into death and into life again that made everything indispensable.

John Joseph and Ashley Reinhardt were navigating through the aisles of a department store north of their hometown, a short drive, and on this day which thrummed with imminent maternity and paternity, a total circumferential idea capturing the pregnant, the items in question are a crib and a stroller, it having been three months since conception; and now in the high ceilinged, linoleum floored department store nothing seemed out of place. All was set in their perfect spaces—the blenders, the clocks, mirrors, mattresses, and refrigerators—and passing these items though not surfacing but lingering perhaps in the subconscious, the thought of purchasing a home welled in John's head, quite a nice idea, he thought, living with Ashley Reinhardt with whom he had gone to school and who was mothering his child. She exercised her thoughts on the subject, living with John, separate from him but alike in the way that by a subtle form of telemetry they communicated and agreed, thinking not of themselves, not of the other, but of the child who was housed in Ashley's bulging belly; having been pregnant with the child in the first trimester was a real experience, something alive and sparkling inside her and which seemed not unconscious but alive and engaging. She smiled thinking about the future, John and herself together as parents as they approached the section of the department store which was particular to baby accessories and flagged down somebody. To their right were wooden cribs and to the left were all sorts of toys and chairs for young children, bouncy chairs, rattlers, stuffed bears, and birds, building blocks on which were painted letters of the alphabet. John by his fiancé's side felt fatherhood beneath him, somewhere in his knees, which had grown weak. He felt woozy but aware, his eyes seeing so much yet taking everything in as if he were taking in small milligrams of liquid light, which filled his heart and his sinuses, his being with a sureness that preceded uncertainty, the question coming to fruition: of this, what will become? Brightness, aid, perhaps. And he noticed he needed a drink. Ashley turned to him and said something unheard. She said again, "John? Are you coming?" To which he nodded his head, following close behind Ashley, quite absorbed.

They had purchased a crib and stroller, had put them in the back of John's truck, and he drove home back to Trolley Court thinking of tomorrow morning's sonogram. The cool blue gelatin covering Ashley's belly was a signature gesture that everything was changing, that all was evolving, and that nothing was to be unchecked, John possessing in the pinkness of that morning, having risen early and having picked up Ashley at her home, a foreknowledge that symmetric parenthood, a mother and a father together visiting the OBGYN and destined to raise a child, was joyous; and he took her by the elbow, guiding her out of the high cab, toward the office, and there was accepted into the bright florescent lights.

Ashley had been having, as most women had when they were pregnant, cravings, cravings for radishes. Many days she stayed with John at the house on Trolley Court and he ran to the store for her.

Once, in the store, John came upon an old acquaintance of his, named Thomas Feldman. John at first did not recognize Thomas Feldman and passed by him in the dairy section of the local grocery store. When they both crossed each other's paths again in the produce section, Feldman spoke up: "John! John Joseph! Good to see you!"

John after a second or two of mental filtration came to recognize his old acquaintance's face. "Feldman? What's up?"

"Oh, you know the drill. How are you?"

John had a bag of radishes in his hand. "Picking up something for the Miss," he said, smiling his innocuous smile, looking at the creases in Feldman's face. He had aged quite a bit in the short years since high school but John did not mind, and John noticed a scar on one of Feldman's cheeks.

"The Miss, huh? Who might that be?"

"Ashley Reinhardt. You remember her? We're going to have a baby."

"Ashley Reinhardt. I remember her." He said this with a gaudy grin on his face that John did not like, but, shifting on his feet, John dismissed the expression with a wave of his hand.

He said, "We'll probably get married."

"Well, I'm glad," said Feldman. He had green and red peppers in his hands and was pushing a carriage full of cola, beer, and rum. "Say, I'm going to have a party, a homecoming of sorts. I've been away for the past three years, up in Boston getting into some pretty shady business but who wants to talk about that? You're invited and so is Ashley."

John did not think a party was appropriate now that

he was en route toward fatherhood, but an inner sense of youthfulness—maybe it was regression back to high school years, he did not know—had him wanting to attend and to bring along Ashley. "I'll think about it," he said, and shook Feldman's hand.

"You know where the place is?" Feldman asked.

"Not a clue."

"Show up Saturday night on Vermillion Lane. There'll be lots of cars. Find a spot and just walk into the house with most noise. That's the house. Hope to see you there."

"Indeed, I may well show up."

"Bye-bye," said Feldman, and turned around his cart full of provisions to continue his shopping.

John Joseph did not know if a party was the best thing for an expectant mother—that she was going into her second trimester warranted a certain degree of rest—but he mused he would talk it over with Ashley as soon as the sun went down, when he would pop open a beer, light a cigarette, and try to entice a bit of the activity in her.

He ran it passed Ashley and it was a go. Saturday night came around and at about seven o'clock P.M. John Joseph turned on the water to take a shower. Ashley, still at her apartment, was waiting to be picked up and taking a shower. Cool water coursed down John's head and onto his chest, which had broadened since the last time he saw his high school acquaintances. He squeezed some shampoo into his hand, turned it into a lather, and washed his hair. He had worked today at the mechanics. He still had a bit of residual grease and dirt on his hands, but after the shower he would be clean for the party at Vermillion.

Dirt dripped from his hands and body into the tub and he moved aside to let the water carry the dirt into the drain. He wanted to go to school. A meagre job at the garage would not support a family; he wanted to look into nursing or culinary. A thinning bar of soap lay on the knee high platform intended for it and he picked it up to wash his face and body.

What did she see in him? They had come together on that night months ago on the beach outside of that bar, but to him it was a matter of circumstances. She got pregnant. That was it. It was not that he did not love her. He fell in love with her that night, he thought, when they were catching up after all those years. She was pretty, tall, had a great laugh—she told him she loved him on countless occasions and he believed her—and that was promising. On that night, there had been no intention of seeing each other again or being together as lifelong partners. But, life had a way of turning him upside down and sending him off, on another track. This, he concluded as he returned the wafer bar of soap back to its place, was the case; and he did not think any less of himself nor any less of her for that matter. It was that now everything seemed so different.

That Grandpa John was no longer around also had a precocious effect on John and he noticed it. Now, he was gone and with his absence there was something of an absence in John's day. This absence did not last all day. It lasted until he went off to work, but when he woke in the morning and went outside for a morning time cigarette and Grandpa John was not there, there was an emptiness. For a time, it had been an illusion. The chair in which Grandpa

John used to sit was empty, but coming from it was a shroud and memory that tended to linger after his death, and that gave John a bit of supposition regarding the ins and outs of life and death. He was no philosopher, but one did not need to philosophize too hard to know that Grandpa John still lived in his heart. Upon returning from work, the chair would still be empty, but a certain coolness emanated from that spot, a certain turning over of a notion that racked John's thoughts, like the crackling of dry leaves. There was no doubt that on Dixon Trail there was a grave with the name John Joseph Sr. over it, but to the young John Joseph, Grandpa John still lived; it was a balance between the believable and the unbelievable that John had to have participated in, a weariness leaving him giddy, a goodbye enticing new beginnings, like a railroad track leading back to the same place. For that reason, John did not mind that Grandpa John was gone. It was the notion that he always was and always would be that gave him the necessary drive to even consider raising a child.

Two nights ago, John had had a dream. Dreams were much of what Grandpa John and young John Joseph talked about, although John Junior was hesitant to let Grandpa John into his haphazard world.

The dream had been in exquisite darkness. John knew he was asleep. He knew he was dreaming. He sensed the house was empty, void of all life but his own. All was silent as snowfall and when John looked at the foot of his bed he saw a shrine of red and gold, a shining stone that towered above the bed and seemed to have consciousness. It was a strange delirium and John knew he would tell nobody about it in fear they would think him mad. But, the dream had occurred and the stone was Grandpa John, the Holiness emanating from the stone a powerful yet subdued niche in thought, through which Grandpa John operated. He woke as words were beginning to be spoken. Waking, he looked at the foot of his bed and saw nothing.

Having a cigarette following that dream never felt so good. He did not know where Jim was, but John knew Jim would be home when he arrived home from work.

Jim brought home a charcoal grill, charcoals, lighter fluid, ground beef, and buns that evening. They grilled out in the back yard, sipping malt liquor and exchanging words that held little meaning compared to the awesome significance of the dream John had had. He said nothing of it. It was beyond context. Not even he knew what it meant, only that Grandpa John had been in that stone. Jim was talking about river pollution when John said, "Jim, what do you think all this?"

"All this, what?" Jim had asked.

"All this. Grandpa John being gone. Ashley and I having a baby. Grandpa Irene getting older."

Jim had not said a word, shrugged and sipped his malt liquor. It was then that John realized Jim was a simpleton. He did not process the uncertain, the uncanny as John did. He did not dream. At least he never talked about them. His life was pretty much set before him with no kinks, no knots in the slack. He was taking his time after Grandpa John went away. Everybody had their different ways of mourning.

John dried off with the towel hanging just to the side of the shower. His skin glimmered. Looking into the mirror, he saw a man that was ready to take the Devil by the balls. He grinned a grin he had not seen in years. It was a grin he had had when he began experimenting with alcohol. He did not know why he grinned that grin, only that it was funny, pervasive, and damned good looking.

Ashley was waiting for him at her apartment. Her belly was starting to show more prominent signs of pregnancy. It did not take too much to convince her to go out, however. She was full of spirit upon the extension of the idea. Then, she had taken a bite from a radish.

She lived a little farther north than Vermillion, so he would have to swing by, pick her up, and retrace his route back to the party. It was no big deal and John preferred having some time to drive and think.

He went into his bedroom, a towel wrapped around his waist, and thought of the conscious stone in his dream. In that space on the floor there was nothing but linoleum and dust bunnies. He stripped of the towel and went to the dresser, put on a pair of paisley boxer shorts, and then went to the closet. He chose a yellow button down shirt and blue jeans. He would wear his loafers.

He gave himself a final look in the mirror, ran his fingers through his hair, and said goodbye to Grandma Irene, who would be asleep by the time he got home—he calculated it would be about two A.M—went out the front door into the cool March evening, and set course north toward his fiancé and the evening's revels. Also, he stopped by the Quik-Mart to get two 32s.

Finding the party was easy. Loud music came from an open front door and there were people all over the front lawn drinking beer and smoking cigarettes. He and Ashley walked inside, John clutching his two bottles of beer and Ashley her belly. Thomas Feldman flagged them down from the living room couch.

"John, Ashley, you made it!" he said, his eyes glazed over.

"We made it, and what a party it is." Over fifty people were crammed into the small home, which was a single story house much like John's over on Trolley Court.

"As I've said, it's a homecoming of sorts. I just got back into town from Boston, where they drove me out like I was a head of cattle. They didn't want me around anymore; I started speaking my mind on subjects I wouldn't want to bore your with, nor would I want to get any deeper into it now that I'm away from the place."

Ashley said, "Thank you." The buzz of the room chattered over the conversation.

"No drinking for you, I'm guessing," said Feldman, taking a step back and looking the pregnant woman up and down, "now that you're preggers?"

"That is correct, sir," said Ashley.

"What'll it be, a boy or a girl?"

"We're waiting to find out," said John. "We want it to be a surprise."

"Well, life's full of those, isn't it?" Feldman said. "I want you to meet someone, you two, come with me." Thomas Feldman led them outside to a packed backyard, where people were playing drinking games and shouting. He walked up to a tall blonde girl and said, "This is Toni, my girlfriend. She's from Boston. She came down with me."

"Toni," John said, "how are you liking Florida?"

"It's a country place," she said, "but I like it. During the days it's quiet and hot and at night people party. In Boston, it's always busy."

Thomas Feldman said to Toni, "Don't tell them why we came back down here okay. I don't want to incriminate myself."

"Gotcha, hon," she said, and pecked him on the cheek.

Feldman left, leaving the trio in the cool March evening.

"Care to have a seat?" she asked Ashley. There was a chair available and Ashley accepted. She sat down and extended her feet.

John drank for a while and they did not speak, listened to the party thrum around them like strings of a guitar. Before he knew it, John was done with his first 32 and asked Ashley if she wanted to go inside and sit at the kitchen table. She agreed, he helped her up by an elbow, and they entered the house.

John opened his second 32. He was feeling drunk by then and a certain good feeling came over him like high tide on the beaches of their small town, where so many times he had bathed, swam, and meditated afterward on the sand, letting the heat and the hot sand bake him into realization. "Good party, huh?" he asked Ashley.

She nodded but did not say anything.

A man beside them, who had been ignoring them turned to Ashley and said, "Ashley Reinhardt? Could it be?"

She turned away, flushed.

"It is you, isn't it. I couldn't recognize you with that belly. I know it's BYOB, but we didn't expect you to bring your own keg."

"Hey," John said. "Take it easy." He eyed this man, who had black hair and brown eyes that were glazed over and red.

"I'll say what I want."

"Not to my girl you won't."

"Excuse me?" said the black-haired man.

"I said, you won't talk that way to my girl."

"Do you know who I am?" asked the guy. "No, I expect you don't. Well, me and Ashley had a thing years ago, didn't you know?"

"Enough, Larry!" shouted Ashley.

"You know this guy?" asked John.

"Yeah, she knows me," said Larry. "She knows me and she knows me well. She also knows me in terms of something southerly."

"Watch it!" said John.

"You know what?" said Larry. "We had it loads of times. It was good, too. Wasn't it, Ashley? And in the first time it was a bloodbath."

John stood up and shattered his 32 over Larry's face. Blood spewed all over the kitchen table. Larry was unconscious. John picked Ashley up by her elbow and headed for the door. He was not going to say goodbye to Feldman and he hoped he would never see him again.

When they were back in the car, John said to Ashley, "We shouldn't have come."

The following day, Ashley was at her place and John

was having a cigarette on the front patio. It was a Sunday and he did not have work. He was enjoying the smoke, pulling it deep into his lungs, meditative on the night prior. That Larry character should not have been talking like that about his girl and everyone knew it. What was done needed to be done.

A white Toyota pulled into the gravel drive of the house. Out came Thomas Feldman. Feldman came over to John and said, "What's up? Can I sit down?"

John gesticulated toward a chair and Feldman took Grandpa John's seat. Feldman was quiet for a moment, a smile across his face.

He said, "Larry's an asshole."

"That he is," said John, who took another deep drag of his cigarette and snubbed it out.

"Why did you do it?" Feldman asked.

"He was talking smack about my girl. I'm not going to stand for that."

"Duly noted," said Feldman. Then, after a moment: "You cut him real bad. He has twenty-one stitches on the side of his face."

"Had it coming."

"I suppose so. He's always getting into trouble and I would have preferred he wasn't there last night," said Feldman. Another pause. "They're coming for you."

"What?" said John. He could not believe what he was hearing. Had he started a war? "What do you mean?"

"After you left and we bandaged Larry up, before he said he needed to go to the hospital, he said he was coming for you. They're coming tonight."

"Really?"

"Really. I'd suggest you skip town for the next couple of days or lock yourself inside."

John was not so much worried about himself. He could handle a few hicks. But, he was more worried about Ashley. "I'll do no such thing," he said.

"Suit yourself," Feldman said. "But, they're coming tonight. He drives a purple Honda."

"I'll keep that in mind."

At that, Feldman got up, nodded, and began walking back to his car.

"Feldman?" John said, as Feldman was walking away. Feldman turned around. "Thanks."

That night, John waiting outside on the patio for a purple Honda to pull up. He had been chain smoking cigarettes. Grandpa John's old rifle was propped up on the building beside him. They wanted it, they were going to get it, he thought. He had no intention shooting the bastard but if that was what it came to John was prepared.

He snubbed out a cigarette and lit another one. It was just past eleven o'clock and John was doubting they would show when a purple Honda creeped up to the house on Trolley Court. It came to a halt and the headlights turned off.

John reached for the rifle not knowing if it would fire. It was an old rifle—John doubted if had been greased in a decade—but he had checked the chamber and it was loaded.

Three men got out of the purple Honda and John noticed they had knives and one had a Louisville Slugger.

"You are as good as dead!" were the words shouted towards the house.

John had made sure to tell Grandma Irene not come outside if she heard a commotion. He had told her some bad people were in the area that night and that it had gotten crazy at the party. John picked up the loaded rifle and walked just beyond the patio.

The fern was swaying in the wind, the flowers danced to an unheard tune, and John waited for them to make a move. When they did, he pointed the rifle at them and they had halted.

"What are you going to do, doofus, kill us?" said the one that must have been Larry. He had a bandage wrapped around his skull.

"I'll kill you if you come any closer."

Larry took a step forward. "Eat it, mother fucker!"

John fired high above their heads. A warning shot. It had fired. He cocked the rifle to ready the second of the two bullets. He did not have to fire. They scared like little squirrels or pheasants, John thought. They ran back into the purple Honda and sped off. They never bothered John again.

John decided not to tell Ashley about the events of that night. He did not want to scare her. She was safe not knowing about such violence and smashing that beer bottle over Larry's head that night in her presence was more than he ever wanted her to see.

Instead, the following evening, he took her to the orange groves just north of town, where orange blossoms lined the verdant fields of South Florida mile after mile. The evening had turned into a mellow ochre and they walked through the trees—Ashley's belly still had not grown large enough to inhibit movement—and John lay down a checkered blanket underneath a water tower.

They sat for a while, drinking juice and eating strawberries when the sun sank below the horizon, the constellations, the moon, and the indigo skies becoming lurid in their eyes, a true Floridian experience—the tress swaying, the cumulus clouds coasting by in harmonious rhythm, the two sharing the time with one another but also with the virility, the rawness of the sub-tropics.

John had finished his juice and put the bottle aside. He lay back, his hands cupped beneath his head as he looked up at the dazzling constellations—there was no light here in the grove—and Ashley lay down by his side.

"Beautiful night," he said.

"Indeed, it is," said Ashley, who rolled over on her side, facing him, picked a strawberry out of the basket and bit into it. "I was thinking," she said, "about finding our own place." She was talking about a place to live but also, to herself, about their place in the world, in life as mother and father. She shrugged and lay back down supine.

"We'll be all right, either way. You can always move in with me for the time being. Jim can sleep on the couch and you can take his bed. Our beds are too small to share. They're twin-sized."

"We should start looking for a place," she said.

He said, "Sure," knowing full well she was ready for the long haul.

She came closer and kissed the corner of his mouth.

She asked him if he wanted to take off his khakis. He did so and John noticed this was her intention the whole time, coming to the grove. She was wearing a skirt, which made easy access, and they were enveloped in hearty fruition minutes later. Her bulging belly was a bit comical to John but he liked it, the extra weight lent by the child inside her, the fullness of her thighs as they straddled him, her voluptuous breasts, which had grown fatter these past few months, readying themselves for the hungry mouths of if not one, two children, who would be amongst them in the coming months. An ebb of surreptitious hotness coursed down his hard part as she climaxed. He pushed through a burst of warmth in his loins and kept on, placing his hands on her buttocks, and pulling. Pregnant, she was infertile and that made things better for him and for her. Seconds followed and stretched into minutes before she reached another piquant thrust. Again, a burst of hotness coursed onto his sack. She had never been like this before but he had heard that pregnant women tend to have a bit more drive next to a woman who was not pregnant. He flipped her over on her back and removed her blouse and brassiere, exposing her breasts, which too were piquant. She was lactating. He bent forward and suckled the juices coming from her nipples, and then he rolled over and relieved himself in the grass of the orange grove.

Dressed again, she lay silent as John smoked a cigarette. He supposed she was speechless—it had been that good for her—and as they lay on the red and white checkered coverlet, basking in the sweet scent, it occurred to John that Ashley was just now finding herself as a woman, that she had an innate beauty in her that was yearning to come out, and that he had granted this to her. He smiled and turned over on his side, asked her if she wanted to go home.

Back at Trolley Court, Jim was in the living room watching television as the two crept into the bathroom and washed each other head to toe, but not before a second round of ecstasy.

They asked Jim if he would sleep on the couch that night. Ashley wanted to stay the night. "Almost prefer it," he said, never taking his eyes from the television. At night, they managed to sleep in one bed, talking in whispers about tomorrow. John, nor Ashley, remembered falling asleep.

He got the invitation bright and early on Tuesday morning. An old friend, Drew Clein, came into the garage looking for a tune up on his old Jeep Wrangler and invited John to come fishing that weekend. John asked if it was okay for Jim to come, too, to which the answer was yes.

Drew made it clear, however, that it was not ordinary fishing—"fishing with a rod and lure is boring," he had said—and that they were going out with harpoons. John was all for it and wanted to witness first hand Drew taking fish out with an outlandish mechanism.

Saturday morning came, and as planned they met at the marina. Jim made sure their cooler was full of goods—ham and cheese sandwiches, strawberries and beer—and they were off at around six o'clock A.M.

"I can take one of you down with me," Drew said. John spoke up first and was given the BC, flippers, and the rest of the scuba gear. "Jim, you'll stay topside and follow this little buoy I have strapped to my BC so we don't get lost."

Jim was snacking on a few strawberries as the trio headed east toward the open water. Rolling crests and troughs of waves jounced off the hull of the twenty foot Boston Whaler. Jim had taken up calling Drew Skipper. "Skipper," he said. "How far out are we going?"

"Not far," said Drew. "Just past the coral reef and the drop off where it gets deeper, where the grouper like to swim around."

Jim nodded his head. He was quite ready for his job, boating and drinking beers. Jim looked back and saw that the shoreline was a painted line of the horizon. They were going out pretty far, no matter what Skipper said. He did not want to start drinking beer too early—it was six-thirty A.M.—but he opened a beer anyway and in a few seconds took it down to the bottom half.

When they reached the area where the grouper swam around, Drew turned to John, who was putting on his BC. Drew said, "Don't have anything shiny on you, do you? Anything that would make you look like a lure?"

"I don't plan on becoming fish bait if that's what you're asking," John said.

Drew laughed. "Just checking."

Presently, Drew leaned back into the Atlantic. John did not have a harpoon. He would watch Drew shoot the fish and hold on to a few of them while Drew snooped around for more. John leaned back and entered the ocean. In a swarthy glush! he was immersed in the water and found the line Drew had casted into the ocean, their line down to its depths. After five meters, John could feel his ears equalizing. He held his nose, tried to equalize. It helped little but he kept descending. Drew was already twenty meters deep by the time John was half that depth. Drew looked up and gave the O.K. sign—index finger and thumb pressed together, the three other fingers sticking out like feathers—and John returned it. He caught up with Drew, who was waiting for him at around twenty-five meters. Visibility was one-hundred percent. He could see nothing but blue in the distance and exhaled a cluster of air bubbles. Further down, he saw a wrecked ship. It was about fifty meters down and Drew once again gave the O.K. sign, which John returned. Drew entered the ship wreck and out swam a Mako shark. John jumped. He had been pretty close. Never before had he see a shark up close. He had heard that sharks bumped into you when they wanted to try you for taste. This shark did not bump into him. It escaped the ship wreck, more scared of John than John was of it. John did not follow Drew into the ship wreck. He swam around the wreck, looking at fish that swam here and there, the green of the algae that had accumulated, the metal of the ship that was now becoming flaked with rust. Drew came out with a grouper hitched to his belt, a bit of blood trailing behind him. John thought that the shark could cut this day short if it wanted, but he pushed the thought away. Drew handed John the grouper. John attached the grouper to a line which was on his waist and had been given him when on the boat. They travelled a bit further toward the coral, and fish and sponges covered it top to bottom, clown fish, lion fish, angel fish, and he marveled at the virginal fish and almost forgot he was following Drew. Red and purple reflected off the coral and into his eye. John thought he should have brought a disposable water-repellant camera. But, this was meant for his and Drew's eyes—he doubted other people came here, dove this deep to fish—and he relished the thought.

Now, Drew shot another grouper, attached it to his hip, and swam over to John. Drew gave John the "let's ascend" sign, an index finger pointed toward the surface of the water. There was little to no drift and John thought Jim had had an easy time tracking the buoy attached to Drew's hip. To avoid the bends, every ten or so meters the two stopped for a minute or two to equalize. Then, they proceeded back to the surface of the water.

Jim was there waiting for them. John and Drew took off their masks and floated in the water. "How was it?" Jim asked.

"It was great!" said John.

"It was fine, just fine," said Drew.

Back on the boat, the two divers took off all their gear and rested a moment before popping open two beers. John checked the clock that was at the wheel. They had been down for thirty minutes. It seemed a much shorter time to him.

"How many have you had?" John asked, noticing that the beer was half gone.

"Not many," said Jim.

"My ass," laughed John, and he was quite all right.

Drew would make a dive, on which John would stay topside, in about an hour. The grouper Drew had shot were deposited in an oversized cooler on the bow. Two big fish.

They almost took up the whole of the cooler. It was noon and they were heading back to shore. Jim took in the Boston Whaler while Drew cleaned the fish, shucked the innards overboard, and divvied up meat for the brothers, ten pounds for each of them.

"Grill or fry the grouper," Drew said, "over a grill or the fryer and bread them, too. That's good eating, and find some tartar sauce while you're at it."

"Will do," said John. He was quite looking forward to the fish. He had not eaten much breakfast. He would grill up some grouper when they got home. Twenty pounds of grouper was going back to Trolley Court. They would indeed be eating good for the next two or three weeks.

There was something about this new item—John and Ashley—that Jim liked, a fresh camaraderie. He stole glances at them at oblique moments, thinking how preternatural love could be, a true folding in of the envelope of life, a crumbling of guardedness and misconception into fruitfulness. Yes, indeed, there was something about it he liked. But, there was also something about his brother and Ashley that he did not like.

He was rooted in stagnation. He had not a girlfriend nor had he a job and he was living day to day leafing through dirty magazines and watching the old television in the living room without content. He wanted to get away. Jim, in all senses of the word, had a certain wanderlust, like a tempest in his gut that drove his imagination over the limits, over the boundaries of the oceans, and brought him to places like Rome, Berlin, London. He wanted to get away, to explore the world unknown to him, and to see with his own eyes the precocious life that flourished in far off places. Sure, he had the Impala, but at best that could bring him to New York City, Nashville. He wanted more. He wanted to hear the broken English of a Spanish girl, struggling to get to know him, because he was good looking and kind.

Was he a token of good faith to his brother? He thought not. But, he also thought, yes. That was exactly what he was.

He was finishing up in the bathroom, one day, when it struck him. When Grandpa John was around and when Ashley was not a factor and taking up all of John's time there was consistency, a certain frequency through which Jim operated as a brother and as a grandson. But, now, there was oscillation in the kindness of Trolley Court. It obfuscated his thoughts and he tended at night to wander through memories of his past, dark and loathsome. He would not again take up the needle nor would he visit that shanty on Goodman Street where one could pay forty dollars for le grecque. No, he would not do any of the sort.

For now, he would lay, think, and meditate on his travels. He had the car. He had a bit of savings that had accumulated over the years after doing odds and ends for a contractor named George Franklin—he despised the work and left it, knowing he was better than lying tiles and applying grout—and would as time came to pass mediate on a flight east, toward Europe and Africa, where he wanted to spend the following year, getting by on hospitable locals, sleeping in hostels, living off the Earth, living for living's sake because that was all he had, consternation in his head that was starting to sound like crystalline chimes.

He thought he would make his move after the baby came—he would not want to miss that—and as John and Ashley came out from the bedroom, Jim lying on the couch watching the television, the precognitive notion came that he would in fact leave Trolley and head east. He would take a plane—by God, he would take a plane—and he would arrive somewhere in the cool reaches of northern Europe and head south to the teeming Mediterranean, would bathe in the sure waters of the mystical element, and fertilize his soul with tidings that came not from the material actuality of the water, but from a place within which no hardships were dealt and no adverse affliction was present.

"Want a beer?" asked John, from the kitchen.

"Huh? Oh. No thanks."

Ashley said, "How are you Jim?"

"Happier than a clam in Biscayne Bay."

She laughed at that, but Jim did not hear it. All he heard was the sound of his beating heart.

The following afternoon, John was grilling grouper on the charcoal grill Jim had brought home. Grandma Irene, Ashley, and Jim were all gathered around watching the fish sizzle.

"This'll be damn good if I don't burn it." John flipped the grouper.

The table out back was set with dishes, forks, knives, and tartar sauce. The fish was just about done when Jim opened a beer and said, "I've been thinking," speaking to John, but the rest were listening. "I've been thinking I might go away," he said.

John turned to him and looked in his brother's blue eyes, a reflection of his own. "Go somewhere? Where will you go? Why?"

"I wouldn't leave," Jim said, "until the baby came—I thought I'd go to Europe—and because it just seems right to me. I want to see what's on the other side of that ocean we always swim in."

"I see."

"I'll have enough money, I think."

"How do you plan on getting the money for airfare? Airfare's not cheap anymore. And hotels? Food?"

"I already have a buyer for the Impala," Jim said, hoping his brother would not be offended. It was his birthday present to him after all.

"The car's yours. Do what you want with it."

"No hard feelings?" Jim said. "About selling the car, I mean."

"No hard feelings. Why would I have hard feelings?"

"You worked hard getting that car in working order," Jim said.

"It's no big deal," John said. "If you want to go to Europe, go for it."

"Thanks," Jim said. "I really appreciate it."

Now, the fish was done and John transferred them to a serving plate that had been in the family for years. They circled around the table, put a slab of grouper on each plate, slathered on tartar sauce, and scooped a bit of coleslaw on their plates, and began eating.

"So good," Jim said, in two prolonged syllables. He thought that fish were somewhere pretty low on the food chain. He, Jim thought, was pretty high in the carnivorous hierarchy. He ate the grouper and tartar sauce, turned to Grandma Irene, and continued the conversation they had been having over the hot grill. "You're not against me going, are you, Grandma?"

She took her time in responding—Jim did not know if it was because her mouth was full or if she did have something against him going—then, she said, "Jim, if your heart wants to travel, your heart wants to travel. Who am I to say differently?"

Jim nodded, said nothing, chewed his grouper, and thought of the next three months when he would be in Trolley Court, awaiting becoming an Uncle, and then the following year abroad. A jovial sense of expectation flittered in his stomach. It was something close to a flock of birds heading south for the winter, only he would be heading east. Overhead, a hawk made its precocious circle, waiting for a rabbit or a coon to come out of its burrow. He thought everything was falling into place. He thought he was on the rise.

Ashley said, "Take me with you?"

"You," Jim said, "have a bun in the oven. Your hands will be full with Gerber baby food, rattlers, and stuffed animals."

"Right," she said.

Jim did not say anything about it, but he had gotten up early this morning and went to the library to look up destinations. One city struck him and he knew it would be the one into which he would fly—Paris, France—and sitting in the seat, in front of that public computer that looked about a cubic foot and half large, he mused on pantomimes, the Eiffel Tower, and renaissance masterpieces. It was a coming together of two worlds—the contemporary American and the woebegone traveler—a dichotomous fissure in Jim that was on the mend. Without impatience, he would wait through the final trimester and then skip town.

It was morning. Julie Ann Joseph was four years old and today was her first day of kindergarten. "I'm excited, daddy," she said. She had been eating eggs and bacon. "I'm really excited."

"Good," said John, "Good. I'm glad."

Ashley was still asleep in the other room. They had acquired their own place just west of the river six months after Julie Ann's birth. A simple two bedroom, one bath, but it was good for a small and growing family.

Julie Ann was just finishing up her breakfast when John poured his second cup of coffee. He had started drinking that stuff like a religion, having given up his job as a mechanic and going to school at the local college. He was studying nursing.

"Almost ready?" he asked.

"Yes," Julie Ann said, and pushed her plate away unfinished. "I'm full."

"Good, that'll hold you over until lunch." John thought of a cafeteria full of children eating lunch, being watched over by the faculty. John told the girl, "We're proud of you. Everybody is proud of you, even Grandpa John."

John had showed a picture of Grandpa John to the girl, a picture taken back in the 1950s, just after he gotten home from Korea. Julie Ann was enthralled. John had said he had gone up to heaven months before she was born. She had asked if he cried when he died. He had said, "Yes, I cried quite a bit."

"Are you okay, now," she had asked.

John remembered the mornings he and Grandpa John had shared, and then said, "Yes, I'm quite well."

John had quit smoking cigarette when the baby came. He did not want to be a bad influence. Smoke around kids and they picked it up, thought it was okay. It was not and John knew it. He wanted to be a good role model for the young girl, and was. "I love you," he said. "Okay, let's go." The father and daughter got into the pick-up truck and headed south toward the school. "Be a good girl today and bring home something nice, a picture or a painting, so we can put it on the refrigerator."

"Okay," she said. She would bring home a portrait of her father, round-faced with blue eyes.

They arrived at the small school, presently. John parked the pick-up truck and walked Julie Ann inside. There were many kids, screaming and shouting. It seemed getting up early in the morning did not faze young children. John and Julie Ann strolled across the cafeteria, which was the rendezvous point for all new students, and went to the table marked with an A-4 sheet of paper on the front of which were taped the letters A-M.

"This is Julie Ann Joseph," said John.

"Well," said a young blonde woman. "Welcome, Julie Ann. We'll get you all sorted out and sitting with the rest of your class in no time." The blonde woman leafed through a few print-outs and found Julie Ann's name and teacher. "Ms. Johnson," she said. "You're going to have a great time with her."

"Okay," said John. "You listen to Ms. Johnson and be a good girl. I'll pick you up around three."

"Okay, daddy," she said, and the two walked over to Ms. Johnson's table, and separated. John gave the girl a hug and a kiss and was gone, knowing full well that this was the beginning of a new cycle if not only in Julie Ann's life in the whole family's. Ashley was waiting for John to come home. She might even be up and out of bed now, but John doubted it. With their second child on the way, Ashley needed all the sleep she could get. And John knew it. He let her sleep in. He got in the pick-up truck and headed back north to where his fiancé—they still had not gotten hitched—waited. Somehow, he doubted they would get around to it before the new child, and doubted if they would at all over the next year. There was so much going on. That sort of ceremony seemed quite removed from reality. Arriving back to their small apartment close by the river, John checked the mailbox and saw that Jim had sent another letter. After four years, he still had not returned from Europe.

John returned to the kitchen table, poured another cup of coffee, and opened the letter. It read:

Dear, John
Back in Paris. London was good. Rainy. Saw Buckingham Palace and strolled through Piccadilly Circus. What a life, huh? Who woulda thunk? Me here in Europe, still, after all

these years, you guys holding down the fort in Florida? Surreal. I've had a hankering for these authentic pastries here they call croissants. The flavor lingers in your mouth at odd times throughout the day. It's a good omen, I think. I'll be here for about a week, visiting a friend, staying with her actually (I wrote you about Claudette before), then I'm off to Barcelona, and then Tangier, Morocco. Haven't yet gone to Africa, and may as well head east to Egypt while I'm there, take a ride over the Sahara. Don't ask how I'm getting the money. It's been a trip. I've been doing odds and ends here and there, promoting books for this publishing company out of Paris all over the continent. It works for me, huh? No plans yet on coming home. I'm just taking it day by day. Will write soon.
Yours,
Jim

John folded the letter and put it in a drawer. The letters were piling up. Jim seemed to be having a great time and that made John happy. That made John very happy.

John went into the bedroom, where Ashley was still asleep. He crawled in beside her. Soon, he fell into a deep sleep. He was on a boat, somewhere off the shores of Florida. Jim was there. It was just the two of them. They were not lost, but they did not have a destination either. There was no land anywhere in sight, but they were happy, the tide lapping the hull of the boat, the air crisp and serene, the gulls overhead squawking.

Ashley, still, was lying in bed beside him. She was awake and looking at him. She said, "You were dreaming."

"I was?" he asked.

"You sure were," she said. "You had a smile on your face."

They lay in bed for a while longer, not speaking but listening to each other breathe. It occurred to John that sometimes when you were lost you were found. He laughed. Ashely's belly was so big. He thought he might just have another two on the way, but that would be as Jim put it—surreal, far too surreal. White wash walls, a queen-sized bed. A wife and a daughter. He thought about making another pot of coffee, but decided against it. This was just too good. He kissed Ashley then and rubbed her belly. John pulled his hand away, turned over on his back, and he heard the trumpet call of a sandhill crane and was spellbound, enraptured, swaddled in a daydream.

Ingenuity

The Abacus, 2400 BC

Smoothened stones on the sands, laid in parallel lines, he uses logic to deduce numbers. It is citrine magic, the notions he has been having, numerals not having been developed yet, and the people think he may be mad, shifting rocks around on the sand alone and listening to the ocean breathe in its shallow rapture; his eyes are wild, he moves with quickness, surefire calculations by the second, by the hundreds and thousands of units—rocks—so simple, this untapped energy seems perpetual and ever-living. He feels a conduit into nature, the sun skipping along the waters and onto his skin and pecking kisses at his forehead, he has found something in this instance, my light having been shed and him having conceived in it.

The First Fully Mechanical Clock, 724 AD

Cogs and wheels, the ultimate machine, the engineer sweats, his fingers dexterous performing surgery. Hovering over him with the ticks of trinkets, his brain activated, is I, the hermit genius, toying with the essence of time with the twist of a dial; he is humbled as I watch and listen to his creation—an intricate layout of brass and quartz—he feels as though he has indeed understood for a long time the intonations of past ages, how they have passed unchecked, unabsorbed, and ill-regarded. In his machine will the day be granted life. And it is endearing how he has come to this present moment, potential deployed in fullness, like wind under a bird; and, ah, yes, here, he does now feel a presence, as if someone is standing beside him.

Eyeglasses, 1280 AD

Pristine edges are cutting precise divisions between matter. There is focus within the eye, the eye clean, and a man feels in this outlandish headpiece sharp, as he holds the contraption to his face with his fingers, it is marvelous how we have constructed such tools. He will show the nobles, they will gape. Vibrant colors defined and hyperemotional when the world had once been ambiguous; he can look everywhere and see with exquisite joy the texture of threads and written language and constellations and the facial features of his family, with exactitude, which have grown foreign in a once-blurred lifetime, now astute; and look, he says, I have even tinted the glass, so we can look at the sun.

The Telescope, 1608 AD

How the sky turns!—the circular momentum of the stars, he can predict where the lights will shift and where they will drop into divine circuit around Earth, where the others will emerge. He is projecting out into the void, where the Moon stands; there he finds in the dashing pin-dots sprawled, a face, indefinite peace, and silence, the celestial masses gliding along the planes of the Gods. Boundless, he is looking and perceives a weightless gift, something which he has been searching for, for ages; he is visualizing, wholesome and wondrous, through the crystal lenses he has sculpted, the face of limitless inspiration. It seems suspended, he thinks—the Moon and the stars—and he is anchored here, though he feels he is in fact with me. He feels he is that much closer, being lifted into the atmosphere.

The Revolver, 1835 AD

Six shots, he spins the chamber. The day is warm and I am not quite sure how I feel about this. This weapon will fit in his belt, be hidden from the world lest he flaunts and wields its power. The chests of men will cave in and blow ragged with lead, many times over; there will be blood, I see, but I am helpless, a mere infatuation. The crafted metal will save lives; it will be the cause of relief as well as pain, and the people watching this demonstration—for he now aims down range, his index finger touching with snugness the trigger—are riveted; and seen by all the men, as well as myself, is the intensity of their intrigue

Antibiotics, 1928 AD

Our bodies are smart, as are the viruses, which sicken it; they will mutate, he knows, floundering, into consequential beings, so small they are not seen, but murderers. He fights them with knowledge and without, with ingenuity; he wishes to save lives with this concoction. It is liquid, and he will direct it into the mouths of men, women, and children, a saint. He will take hands into his own to make sure the sicknesses do not gain grounds, because he is the barrier between life and death, the apex of understanding, the first to recognize that things may turn bad, that things may end; perhaps these children will live a complete life, perhaps not; he can only imagine what will happen tomorrow, when he brings the medicine to the first of the families, who are waiting in ill-tempered homes, waiting for tomorrow as well.

REM-T, 20— AD

The night falls, as it has many times before. She is upstairs, weeping into her pillow. The white cotton has turned gray because of her tears and her cheeks will wet when she rolls in her sleep. And there I will be waiting for her. Where the times can turn and where she may cast spectral colors into herself, a rainbow upheld by her own consciousness. The dream she will have tonight will change her; I have administered three droplets of my solution into a glass of water, which she has drank. She will be asleep in minutes. I hope to all that the solution will affect her; I have tried it on no one but myself. And it had worked! It had worked, I tell you, and I met the very thing that has driven me to this completeness I feel now: hope, dreams, and color. We will wake tomorrow beside each other in the same bed and she will remark, What an incredible dream, what an incredible morning! And I will lie, quiet and smiling, listening to her song and listening to the water in which she bathes dripping and listening to my muscles vibrate, listening to hers do the same, pretending I am still asleep, musing that she, through her bright path of a sleep, has discovered all that there ever was to know—

A Beautiful Tyde

Chuck Palmer dances across the street toward East Sachson, jubilant in his thin underarmor shirt and slacks. He has decided, They are good people. That they live forever in the mural does not mean that they are perfect, but those on the walls—those people on the mural, illustrated by tiny squares of tile and distinguished by strips of vertical and horizontal intersecting grout—are handsome.

The half a dozen men on the wall in Downtown Sachson are immortal and handsome. It is like these people could just walk right off the tiles and onto the street and get a cup of coffee, growing into four dimensions and live. Just past the small pre-school, past the Formatta Teahouse on the right, across the street from church, which follows the Teahouse, Chuck Palmer dances up to a house where they live, a house with small palmettos and children's toys strewn across an un-manicured lawn.

A man answers the door, to whom Palmer introduces himself, and the man who has answered looks at this Palmer estranged, wondering why and how this man has found him, because it is not like anyone knows he is here, why he is here. He is stumbling.

"Name's Palmer," Palmer says. "Chuck Palmer."

The Black man says, "Tyde," holding out his hand.

Chuck Palmer chokes on his words, looking for breath in which to speak so he can say, "I've found you!" It seems this man, this Tyde is pulling at Palmer's skin. It is tightening. It is like Tyde is something higher. And behind Tyde is a sliding glass door, across the living area, across which a reflection is being casted around Tyde like a white and blue corona, contrasting the light mocha of the man's skin, Tyde, who is remembering, This is my home and why is this man here? Palmer states, "I'm interested how you've achieved your success," thinking he is ready to learn.

Tyde replies, "Why are you here?"

To which Palmer says, "Do you know how to fish?"

To which Tyde says, "I know how to fish, and you have to get out of here, sir," closing the door.

Palmer, in his slacks and smooth collared shirt and clean skin, stops the door from closing with a palm thrust, and says, "Tyde, you are a beautiful man." Tyde looks at him and shakes his head, thinking, Wow, this is the country we live in, and as he closes the door, he watches Chuck Palmer's eyes slip away back into themselves.

The porch is dirty, long beams of wood comprising the deck on which Palmer stands much too long. Tyde is watching him through the slit venetian blinds, behind the walls and the translucent windowpane, which has not been cleaned in months, in the protection of his own home, where he and his family have lived for years. He watches Chuck Palmer turn and walk away, down the street toward the river and Downtown Sachson. Chuck Palmer is walking over the child toys strewn on the lawn and from the back

Tyde can see the tattered hem of his pants and the wrinkled fabric of his shirt and the mangy hair on his head, and he calls over his daughter, this Tyde, and says, "Look girl, see that man? Handsome isn't he?" He paused and said, "A very handsome man."

Equal Men

Separating two worlds, the old and new, the staircase one last time is mounted by Richard Louis, walking into his retirement. The old man feels it in his legs, the staircase rescinding his weight; and upon taking that last step sees his son, who is waiting for him; the chiseled face, which has not changed since childhood gazes upon his in admiration. Two men, having met, shake hands, a father and a son, in total peacefulness; and yet, there is apprehension. The old man, Richard Louis, is retired, having left that workplace. They have met in the mouth of the subway; and they are granted a look at one another, a opaque glance, which transports them back to steadier times and when times looked less drab. A time of uniting is at hand; and upon shaking hands, they exchange greetings in simple words, which mean little beside the grand features and formalities by which they have known each other for so long, a father and son in harmony.

Greetings.

Goodbyes.

The couth undertone of winter is imminent; they feel each other's body heat through their thick coats and take a step synchronized in a direction, which feels irregular; an anomaly has descended: the warmth, cushioned by sharp winds and the cracking cold, which sets them Earthed. A sprouting or V-shaped branch is a way they feel, like a moose with its heavy head pulling him towards water and nutrients. Today is a day for celebration because the old man has retired, a splendid bout of upwards of sixty years working in the city as an architect. The young man has wished he followed in his footsteps; and yet, the content young man, the son of Richard Louis, takes lead in the short -lived moment of lucidity, which preludes the starting of a motor. The child and father relation has been mediocre at best, with the frill edges of temperament coaxing an otherwise stellar relationship.

The temperament has been roused by years of unnecessary council; because father knows best, son is always at a loss, at a loss for words, at a loss for emotions; and yet, by the finality of everything, there is a pot of gold, savings having been stored away, like a bear steals away meats and fish into his gut, in this season, and then caves in for hibernation.

It is pure and instinctual. A bear recedes into its den as a man does his bar, on a day such as this, says the son of Richard Louis. A day like this is a day one celebrates. It seems the tables have turned by means of a daring poltergeist—the son advising the old man and cajoling him out for a night on the town, which is filled with beer and wine and tasty bowls of snacks and women and youth. As the car starts and pulls out from its parking space, which is beside a curb and a parking meter, the son forgets his manners, does not bite his tongue and says, We're going out tonight. It's a business casual place. You're dressed well as it is. We'll make a stop by my place, so that I can get dressed.

Business, thinks the old man, is at an end. With this publicized deficiency of openings for jobs and the growing demand for foodstuffs and disability checks it's a wonder I'm retiring at sixty-five. He questions himself, feeling older than he is, sixty-five?

The mind crosses into inheritance and paperwork. Richard Louis is composing his will, in mind—the ethereal place where thoughts can happen on their own accord or on a whim, like a twig falling to the Earth, indenting the snow. The light impression given by the notion is none too far from disconcerting. There is the house, the car, the savings, the valuables, watches, rings, and jewelry. There are the books. The countless books, which compile Richard Louis's library—the high bookshelves filled with novelists like Fyodor Dostoyevsky and Jules Verne. Richard Louis almost brings it up, his son's inheritance, but drops the topic like a rusty penny in a fountain. They are approaching his son's home, a modest two story home with a green rooftop coated white by snow.

Richard Louis has always enjoyed that rooftop. It is a vibrant green, not the standard forest green, but a lime green like the leaves of a young oak tree, yellow-green.

Two men, separated by the apparatus that clinks and toils when it changes gears, remove themselves from the car. Approaching the house, the silver ground crackles under their feet. Crisp breaths are taken through the old man's nose; and he is sharpened by the bite of the season. It is a pleasant bite, like the bite of a teething puppy dog.

Musing, the old man thinks, Glad I never got one,

referring to dogs. A twig must have fallen. Because of the nostalgic day, the end of workdays, inheritance comes to mind, once more; but it seems his son has inherited all that is of value, already, the musing Richard Louis thinks, thinking of the personality.

His son seems to be doing well. He has always had a good head, but he can remember a few times it got the best of him. Richard Louis eddies away from the thought.

The décor of the household is quite nice—maroon drapery, white carpets—and the old man is offered a drink upon entering the house, to which he declines the offer. He is not thirsty.

There are so many similarities between father and son, the high cheekbones for one, the eagle-like nose, and brown eyes, the careful arches of their eyebrows and big ears. The creases at the corners of their eyes, of which Richard Louis has more, that sets them apart, that and their intrinsic views on the world. Richard Louis has been okay with his small house—a single story house, with two bedrooms and one bathroom, a small modest white kitchen with a homey little living area separating the bedrooms and the kitchen. He decides to step outside, into the frosty outdoors. The street is quaint. The lawn underneath all that snow must be manicured. The fence is taught. The trees lining the street stand like men in a queue at the soup kitchen. He can almost see them exhaling their oxygen; and he takes a breath, admires his breath. It is much like a cycle. One gives, one receives. Only it is better to be on the receiving end.

On top of all the years past, Richard Louis has retained class. Receiving many a joyous night with candor is like a cup of warm milk; he relishes his memories before bedtime and those memories lull him into sleepiness, which he values much like a bear values a river full of salmon; they swipe in with their claws and withdraw their meal. The only topic that does not lull Richard Louis into his sleepiness is the thought of his wife; he is a widower as of late. His wife has died five years past and he can still remember the texture of her stockings, the way she washes herself in the evenings, and scents of soap in bed, the way her softness takes him, propels him into the armpits like a hound in a fox's den.

There is a fireplace in their old house. The chimney reaches up to the rooftops and expels white smoke. Richard Louis's son asks how Santa Claus fits in the chimney, how does he get all the way down? The answer is one word—Magic. Escaping the lips of a mesmerized father the word sounds like a magical cue, which renders the young boy into reverie; and awe takes prescience. The boy sleeps with the image of cookies and milk set out for the fat man who shimmies down the chimney once a year on the twenty-fifth of December. Every year it happens and the young son is hypnotized by the notion—the North Pole, the elves, the fat man who rides a sleigh around the world in a few short hours.

Now, the notions are few and far between. The young boy has grown and learned that it is a myth; but something in the daring young man has him thinking that myths have a source of realism. They have emanated from somewhere, inspired by a partial-truth, a quasi-reality, which adorns the minds of the old and young. This is the way the imaginative mind is composed.

Now, the poles have him curious to a different effect. It is the polar shift, which enamors the young man with riveting thoughts and conversation at the evening celebration. The conversation is one of natural disasters and the polar shift. The climates will have exchanged places, like body heat in a cold-blooded animal.

Age, however, does not change places. It is a steady stream of consciousness. It goes in a straight line or a circular trend, cyclical, if one believes in that circle of life hogwash or the completion. Richard Louis deviates from the conversation, his thoughts touching back on soot and Santa Claus and the holiday season. Even the sun feels cold on a day like this; he does not feel its warmth in the afternoon. It is cold and electric. He feels a comparable aspect to his own son, in this case. The young man has left the old man out of the conversation, not with intention, however, just as the sun on a winter day does not intend to be cold. He is feeling less and less welcome.

All the man wants is to exchange a good word and return home a retired man, and relax as does a retired man. Moreover, what wants to be exchanged are the rudiments, the rudiments with the refined, a bum with class, thinks Richard Louis, self-depreciative. A token evening is one part of the grand scheme. What is the young man doing with his father on this night? It seems it is a token, like one receives at an arcade. One deposits a token into the machine and there is a time of entertainment. The game carries on and ends.

Recalled is the handshake upon entering this restaurant. Richard Louis has shaken hands with a man solid in his frame, with a firm handshake, broad shoulders and done-up hair; and its like his handprint has been scanned, like a Morphotank in a jail, the impression never-ceasing, the handprint never failing to bronze up any impression given by the old man. He has reached his Golden years in a machine state.

Talismans, brass rings, shoe polish retain most of the human being today. Richard Louis feels his gut has become brazen in the circumstances; his shoes have become too small, the toes may burst out the fronts like a clown's. Somebody says something but it goes unheard. It is directed towards him; and he flinches, snorts in agreement.

He will write a book in retirement. Pages on pages of narrative and prose to go along with the mundane happenings of old age; but is it so mundane? The sharp air of winter keeping the lungs alive, the lucky sun in the height of the afternoon, a whiff of acrid smoke in the city. All keeps ends on edge.

Without a word, Richard Louis steps toward the restroom. He is mere inches from his reflection he is mere inches. Perhaps it is best to reconcile with himself before venturing into his son's heart. It is almost time to go when he returns to the table and finds himself wanting to trade jackets with his son. Similarities are what he finds in the two jackets, but if he suggests this they might think of him as a zealot.

They have gone on their pilgrimage into the city, visited in original attire the setting of old and new, old and young, brought together, like a museum and its visitors. Richard Louis is satisfied, but taking the boy on a tour through his memories is what he wants, to coast through panes of glass and windows and lenses so that he can view how he, Richard Louis, thinks; but there is the tied down effect, the part where his son knows all and what can the old man teach him at this point? Something about desire.

There is a hill down which they navigate on the way to the subway station and back to the city minor. Richard Louis pretends he has gone skiing—he never has—but he is good at it; he races down the hill on skis. The city is melting in his vision and, slow, they descend into the subway station, spelunking, or otherwise zipping through the cavern, with fervent legs, feet, anticipation, skis.

Deepness is found in that subway, deepness like in the ocean or deepness like in the snow or deepness like in an inhalation or a gulp of beer. The spicy scent of the subway takes the two, father and son, father apart, yet closer. They are sitting beside one another, thinking of each other.

Retirement is like birth thinks the aging Richard Louis. It is like he is seen a new light and he is excited to go home. His bones are chilled, all the way from the skull to the humorous, chilling, to the radius and ulna, all the way down his spinal cord, to his coccyx and femur and tibia and fibula. The metatarsals are begging for a hot shower. The metacarpals in his hands asking for the hot water. His son, on the other hand, is all muscles, all the way down from the trapezius, down the latissimus dorsi, to the gluteus maximus, medius, and minimus, enamored by fanaticism; but it is Richard Louis who feels out of turn. His old bones are feeling brittle and his muscles are feeling tattered and his spirit is feeling insubstantial; and his son is walking with such sureness, smartened at the lashing cold, fastidious. Equality is all Richard Louis wants, to be equal, not young like his son—he has been that age already—but to know what he is thinking. He wants a piece of his mind; he wants to know how he feels on this evening, because it is an evening of importance. However, it seems it has fallen into commonality. They split in a second, like a hairline fracture. The explosive schematics of the relationship shows all the bones, all the muscles torn apart, in the eyes of Richard Louis. Equal men, that is all he wants; he wants to be equal men, strong men, while they are eating food and chewing and creating energy in their brains, which is composed of gray matter and electricity. It must run cold.

Richard Louis has thought before how captivating the human body is. It eats and from that food creates in the brain electricity; the brain via this electricity tells the muscles to contract and move the bones in a direction, so that the body can move; it is like magic, an incredulous organism. One eats, and then tomorrow one moves; it is surprising there is not a carrot dangling before their heads, but there must be, on some electromagnetic and ethereal level of vision. There is that much irony.

The hairs on Richard Louis's head are like tilde symbols reaching out looking for an extension or an absolute value. Questioning his son, he says, Had a good time tonight? His tone a bit vivacious, ironic, but predestinate.

He seeks to balance the equation. Calculus is not his strong suit, but it might be easier to get through to a derivative than it is his son. Genealogy and pedigree are more so the topic in question; and it does dawn on him that they are different men. They are in two different places and the same time. It is not like he is a practiced Buddhist, able of being multiple places at once, banging a drum in one room while meditating in another. He removes a comb from his pocket and parts his hair. Equal men. Different men. Is there a difference? There must be, because when he thinks of himself as an equal man he feels vibrant, a shaking in his feet and arms, like h is nervous; but he is not. Anew is the proper way of putting it, anew and aging. Richard Louis is longing to return to his own settlement. His cold skin pulls him towards the car, a diversified vessel, an instrument of motion, as opposed to stasis, like a Longhouse or a Hogan or an Igloo.

They arrive. His small house is yearning for Richard Louis to enter, start the fireplace, have a cup of coffee, and sit down and read. Before exiting the vehicle, Richard Louis turns to the left, shakes his son's hand and says, See you later, which he does not say with anticipation. It is a melancholic tone of voice. He refuses to say thank you. He exits the car and faces his son through the frosty window, and then it dawns on him that this is the last time they are together as equal men.

On His Way to Elysia

Now, they have wrinkles, blemishes on their skin, and bags under their eyes. Here, in this concrete jungle, this twisted metropolis made up of red bricks, phone lines, and cracked concrete, they have aged. They have been here for years. "Too many years," says Lewis, his eyebrows loose and patient, while his love, Marge, brews espresso on the stove. "Way too many."

It is nighttime.

She has said it many times before. "Lewis, you want to leave?" she asks. "And where will we go? Back to Greece? The place is a free-for-all. They're stealing from the museums, Lewis, staling their own past. I'm ashamed, Lou, ashamed."

She says this again, clutching two cups filled with coffee, and Lewis knows the coffee will be perfect because it is like she can read his mind, read how much sugar he wants, how sweet he wants his coffee. Three teaspoons of sugar she spoons into his cup and sighs, "ashamed," as an afterthought; and he takes a sip. It is perfect.

He is aging, he knows. He is eighty-four and tomorrow is his birthday.

The future has been pulling at him, like thread. He

can feel the pulling above his crown, like a calling from angels. "How many years do we have left, Marge?" he asks, but she does not speak.

Far off, the shallow rushing of cars breathes on.

Two eggshells broken on the counter lay peaceful. It is morning, Lewis's birthday, and she pours into a pan more olive oil. "Scrambled, eh, Lou?" Marge asks, already beating the eggs.

With the arms of an antique clock ticking away, reading 5 A.M. above the window, Marge says, "Happy birthday."

"It is my birthday, isn't it?"

"It is," she replies.

They stay in the kitchen, Lewis reading his paper, looking at an advertisement for a cruise ship. It is in color, so the ship pops off the page; and Lewis cannot imagine how big the ship really is. It is hard to tell just by looking at it. There is nothing beside it to gain perspective. The ship is just floating in the water. Ships are entertainment when they used to be transportation. Immigrating here, spending five weeks on a ship and crammed together with people you did not know, eating bread and salty rice and undercooked potatoes day in and day out leaves a bad taste in your mouth. He would almost rather swim.

"Here, Lewis," Marge says. "To many more." She is holding out a cupcake with a lit candle in its center.

"To many more," he replies, blows out the candle.
He envisions different places, which have escaped him in his life, places he has not touched, and some places he has touched. The wheat fields through which he used to run and

work; mountains upon which he used to gaze; the cruise ship; the printed water in which the ship floats—all seep through his eyes and into his stream of memory, like water through a sieve, and leave him at his kitchen table.

Marge's large face is smiling down at him, with soft eyes that look almost concerned. She is scared. So am I, he thinks, and his heart swells with her breath. We are here in the dark, and she will stay here until the stars fall. She will not move. And again I am promised the future and I hear, Could this be my last?

And then, he does make a wish—the beach. He wants to see the water; he wants to be in the water. He wants to feel himself become absorbed by the ocean, its suppleness receiving him, the salt water like cotton swabs on his skin, cleansing him, washing him.

Stepping from the kitchen table, he is on his way out the door when he catches a glimpse of his wife's green eyes, eclipsed beneath half-slit eyelids; the beach is shimmering behind her. She is standing on the sand; and her feet are sandy. Plants sprout beside her. Shrubs and seaweed wash ashore in a crescendo of willpower. He wants to swim. Pink crabs sidestep in front of her and sunshine has spread across her back, her face at an angle that makes her skin look divine. The image is lingering as he breaks through the first wave. He has left his wife in the kitchen, and he, waist deep in water, is growing into the vast blue plane. He has left her without a word, only a look, knowing their time together has come to this place—the beach, him in the water and Marge behind him, her toes buried in sand.

He is swimming and the shore is a painted line on the horizon.

"Have you heard of Elysia, Marge? The place where the heroes go?" He is thinking between his swimming strokes. "I am no hero, but I am searching anyway. Maybe I will find it. Maybe I will find where the gods have placed our childish dreams, somewhere deep in this ocean. I am striving, my dear wife, and hoping that you take your time in finding me, where I've gone. As I swim through these troughs and swells, I'm reminded of what I've left behind—you and other things, which are important. But not as important as this moment." He belches swallowed water. "The most important moment of my life," he says. "Just know, Marge, that I have never felt more alive."

The Column of Air

Jessica bows her head and spits in the sink, looks into the mirror. A thousand different thoughts have come to mind, sparks ricocheting from her eyes, a thousand different vantage points, areas of conquest, tribulations, triumphs. She splashes water in her face. Silver lining has always been a dream, and liquid. Liquid: what flows underneath the volumes and volumes of human emotion. And underneath that: fire.

Light blue water dribbles down her chin as she washes her face, with soap. The suds stick to her cheekbones like tape, slide down like windblown tickers in an alley, reading different tones and shades. Blue ice enters her brain—the water is freezing. In fact, she cannot imagine what can be colder on a morning like this one, after a night of fun, a greasy dinner, a club, and what came after—the fire—and the dense and trapped flame, the temptation, the anger, the consequential effect of a thought borne wrong, in a wrong world, at the wrong time. Outside, the church bells toll.

For the first time in her life she is moving outside the city limits. It is not much the anticipation, or the harpsichord tunes, that are escorting her mind to this forsaken corner of thought. It is the thought that she may not return.

The time grows later, but seems to stand still, but at an elevated height. Time must be on a vertical axis. It does not go forward. If anything it goes in. Into the heart, into the belly, into where the flame exists and where the mind churns, grows, emulating thoughts and feelings. Today she leaves, and today she flies.

Gray walls and coffee shops have kept the young woman here in a stasis, the appreciating beauty that has grown on her, like mercury in an ocean. Surrounded by water, she breathes; she calls, builds golden bridges over waters, existential blades of grass.

A thermal is what she needs, but the wind here keeps her anchored. An upward draft, a spiral of piping hot air, rising, up above the tree line, above the concrete and metal framework, over the mirrored buildings that reflect her body, up over the rails, where time travels lighter.

She can feel it, the moist crocheted clouds as she dries her face, willowy. She will remark at the birds flying there, through where time, as she sees it, will take her. But it burns, the flames from last night, and the short notice, and her fortress, gone, now a homemade of water. What will take her to the new place, outside the limits, her companion and life, shine pearls, in her whispers.

She places down the hand towel, returns to her bed, pulls out the duffel bag from underneath her bed, musty and brown. Right through her city, her desire is dispersed by a column of air—rising, rising.

Washing her hands, she stands and looks herself over in the mirror. They are still there, the pockmarks, the swollen glands of her tear ducts, the thin and cleaned eyebrows, tweezed and glossy. And there, just added are the streams of emotion running from her eyes, her awareness of her age.

There seems not to be an end to all these thoughts, these feelings, ever-gliding, eroding the beaches and riverbeds of her old life. They are still there, the tears and her imagination, all too resplendent to be forgotten, but livid, bucking like a wild animal, needing to be released into an eternal world and clean air and a breathable existence. On this day it is easy for her to keep the emerald energy afloat. It is easy to see her reflection. It is easy not to hear whispering words. For today, she is leaving. Today, she is taking it for granted, this life, these thoughts, these welling, budding tides of emotion, which spiral to the top of her thoughts and energy.

There is an open window.

And the Bohemian sun shines through, the days hot. Looking through the window, time is omnipresent. Stretching out into the everlasting plane, her vision is carried away by the birds overhead, the clouds above theirs. A past life.

What is a past life? A dormant pocket of psyche. Dormant until roused in a vision or a dream. What is a past life? A forgotten smidgen of truth or the coughing notion of desire. What is a past life?

To her, it is the air. The knowledge that whatever has happened is only an illusion—an illusion taking the form of evaporation. Finding the spaces in between knowledge and foreknowledge in which to live and relax for a moment, in between the particles, the atoms, where the real magic occurs, is tantamount. It is real attraction.

And here, she is taken by a knock at her door. The hotel is bountiful. She has won a prize. A sweepstakes that has brought her to this forsaken island, save the water, to learn the art of yoga and appreciation albeit alone and without a master. The only master is the one in the reflection. However, underneath all that skin and hair and organic flesh and water, is more. A backdrop of the real Jessica. Behind the scenes. A backdrop made of light and emotion. Another knock.

She answers and the man who has been knocking has pockmarks, swollen glands, thin and cleaned eyebrows, easy and tweezed.

The window to the crown, a knock in her chest. She recognizes this man. Jessica takes a breath, wipes her water from here face with her sleeve, looks behind her, through the open window upon the turquoise waters, which will never ever be the same, never be different, always alike in one regard—they will always support life and the endearing fortune of it. She reads the clouds at a distance, hears the birds, distinctive. And a word trickles, having been let out, trembling, a word that has escaped from her interior dam of emotion, trickling, "Hello? Do I know you?"

Eight Minutes to Thanu

Chaos is sharp, but so is Mortimer Goldberg on the last day of his life. Mortimer dreams of the birth of his first son and Garbanzo beans and the circles of Hell. All the states of matter together at once, he realizes, is consciousness.

To relinquish: verb, to renounce or surrender re·lin·quish
re'liNGkwiSH/
to relinquish the throne

Mortimer Goldberg has ricocheted up and over the hood of an oncoming Chevrolet. Gliding past cars, sirens screaming, Mortimer Goldberg and his mother are growing closer.

Pigeons and bells are circling above his crown. Mortimer's brain bleeding. All facets expunged, except mortality.

Thanu.

Zipping passed trees and clouds and asteroids and comets are Mortimer Goldberg's ideas. All essential energies are being pulled from the body and into the crown. In the hearts of the two—Mortimer Goldberg and his mother—a likened resolution has been found. The exchange has taken place in the heart of the city; and his two eyes are closed, the third open.

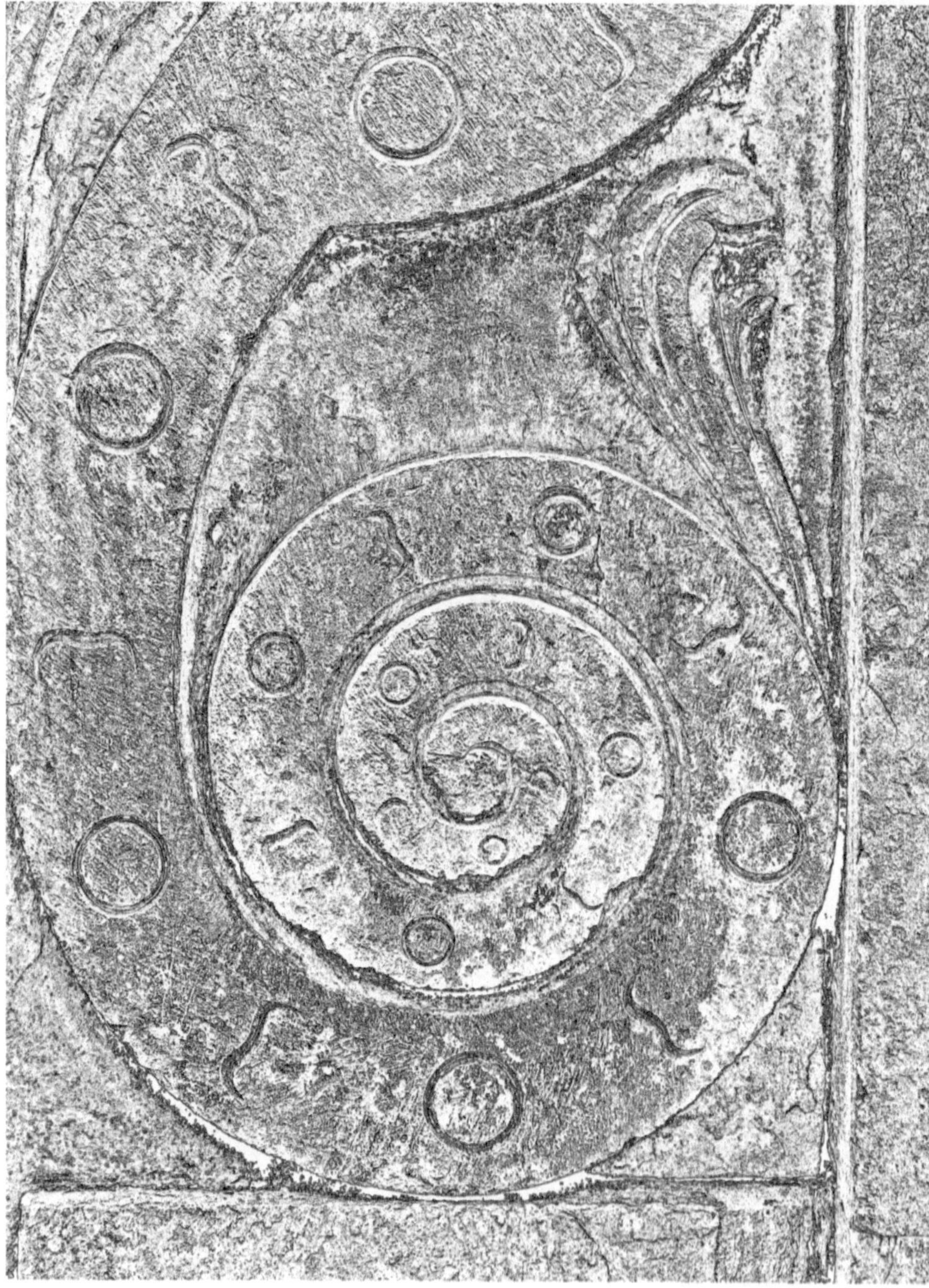

Engine Trouble

Two brothers are picking up their father at the airport. In the lackadaisical mid-morning heat, they coast down the highway, disconcerted and on edge. They have not seen their father in years. The man has relinquished any pleasure in the form of children. He has lost that element. The thrumming of the engine gives under the weight of abnormality. For is this normal? An elder son and his brother seeing their father for the first time in a decade? They feel the tentative thought giving way, underneath their legs; and in this time they decide to take him out for a cup of coffee, having agreed this is the first time in years and the very last time they are seeing him.

Mother has died; and she is not coming back, and father is coming only to collect.

Collect what? Their thoughts on the matter, which have collected in a puddle around their mother's ankles, like dirty dishwater and fibrousness? The crystalline morning is lacking, in the way of identity.

The morning identifies with the people. The people do not identify with each other. It is for this reason the brothers are on edge, in a place between comfort and the uncouth. He has always been liberal—liberal sprinkling of salt on his food, liberal taking of what he wants.

They are looking forward to the goodbye—an impersonal separation of blood. Some genuineness will trickle over, maybe. If not, the day will crumble, like crackers in soup.

He enters the car, says, "Hello." They shake hands, like men. The radio is on and is quiet. They wait for a word, but it never comes. At noon, they go for coffee. Weighed down are the feet of the brothers. Light and on edge does the father feel. They sip hot coffee. They wait. They wait for the cue to leave, to get back in the car and descend to quasi-normality.

It is in this stasis that a son says, "Welcome home."

"Home is in Kentucky," says the father.

"Indeed," says the eldest son.

They have coffee cups in the cup holders, angst is in the engine, folly is in their hearts.

Young Lovers

He first saw her during coffee hour, in the Catholic church on Second and Thirteenth. She was filled with spirit, mass having been just finished. She wore her golden cross outside of her beige vest. She approached him and walked passed him, saying nothing. This was the moment he saw her. This was the moment he fell in love.

In repose, he dreamt of her smooth skin and the way her hair was loose. He lost sleep; he day-dreamed; Mauricio Alvarez thought not of business, school, or otherwise, only of Demartez.

He as of yet had not learned her name. This was a confounded realization. He attended mass the that Sunday, followed by coffee hour in order to learn her name.

She was present, as he had hoped. Her hair, loose, tousled, and to the right side, was brown as he remembered. She wore purple today, an airy shawl, reminiscent of lavender in spring. She entered and looked both ways. Mauricio caught a glimpse of her profile. A healthy, round face, with sunken temples and a prominent chin. This was when he grew scared. He grew scared not of rejection, but of his own manliness. He was seventeen and tall, with patchy scruff under his chin. He thought she might be attracted to men, not boys.

She thought of him a man. He had introduced himself as Mauricio and took her hand in his and kissed it. She smiled and turned red.

At twenty-four years old, she had still not found a proper man. Mauricio knew this. She had told him one evening. They were at the beach. The breeze blew, gentle, and the waters surged, powerful. Sand stuck to their feet and in between their toes. They sat and watched the moon rise high into the sky and told one another of secrets they never before shared.

She was scared of the sea. Demartez told Mauricio she was scared of what she could not see.

"So," he said. "You're scared of the dark?"

"No," she said. "Just the things I cannot see."

"What's the difference," he said.

"Scared of the dark is one thing," she said. "The dark can't hurt you. What hides in darkness can." She sat on her buttocks, in the cool sand, leaning back on her arms. Her legs were extended.

Mauricio said, "Come into the water with me."

"It would be cold, no?" she said.

"Not too cold," he said.

"Okay, but stay close to me."

Mauricio agreed. He felt ambivalent and triumphant. He removed his shirt and khakis, and she removed her dress. They entered the water and let it crash on their bodies. It was cold and Demartez hissed between her teeth. Mauricio took her by her arms and guided her deeper into the water.

"It's been ages since I've been in the ocean," said Demartez.

"I'm glad we're together," said Mauricio.

They kissed then, under the starlight. In the darkness of the water they kissed. Demartez was not afraid. She felt secure. Never had a man touched her like that.

Mauricio guided her back onto shore. They lay in the sand and kissed. Then, Mauricio's hand went low and touched the puffy part of Demartez's underwear.

"Yes," she said.

It was cold out of the water. Mauricio was having trouble. His temper was rising. He had not the gravity a man would have under the circumstances; and he cursed under his breath.

"I'm not able," he said.

"Why not?"

"I'm not able," he said.

He was frustrated and put on his clothes. They sat beneath the starry sky and spoke with lightness.

"I was being impatient and ugly," she said. "I'm sorry.

"That's okay," he said, and he doubted another opportunity would arise. He was angry and considered himself a boy.

"Maybe another time?"

"You're instigating this," Mauricio said.

She said nothing more and looked ahead toward the horizon. She had never had a man. She wanted one, desperate. After Mauricio had arrived she wanted one, desperate. She wanted a man with strong arms. She wanted a man, desperate.

Mauricio was thirsty. He had not brought anything to drink. He did not care how Demartez felt. He did not care if she was thirsty.

Aurora Sunrise

Impossible was not a word used by Javier Ricardo, and he mused that impossibilities were the possibilities of the future—other Javier Ricardos in entirety, who metamorphosed the dreary and impossible into the dazzling and prodigious. He played a broken guitar. He serenaded Angelic listeners who lingered over the horizon. Eastward his thoughts gravitated. Its red-golds, airiness, and brazen light granted a piece of that miracle known as foresight; he saw the impossible being enacted; he smelled the cooking of beans and chicken; and he saw the flares of age and all proclivity regarding psychic awareness. The past masked the present with a veil of secrecy, which none other than magic could dissolve. Javier Ricardo procured dawn with tawdry notes and forlorn tones; and also practiced magic. Were there requisites for entering hallowed agedness? Were there dangers that preluded that eventual jaunt into the everlasting? He neglected his fear of such things as loneliness and malcontent.

He would visit the lake.

Trees glowed in effervescent beauty as thirst took him. He would drink of the lake. The water was clean and still. Still enough to catch the feigning reflection of his face in the ripples. Cascading from the trees was verdant green—as per the ascending and translucent sun and rays, which hovered and cascaded equal, yet complimenting, colors. A lark dove from a tree. Phantasmal redness traced the bird's flight; and the bird dipped passed Javier's head. The bird had left behind it a color. And, as natural as it had come, Javier Ricardo accepted the phenomenon as a part of that magic. He took a deep sip of water from his cupped hands—Angelic, a corona predominated his head, and lent perception to brilliance. Yellow and thick, the water put off—perhaps it was an illusion—a distinct idea that he was supernatural. Hardened by time, he solidified, as in a kiln, and he aged before the lake's bank. Extraordinary! Arriving in youth and leaving with clarity, blemishes, and bags under his eyes.

Javier Ricardo lived with such fullness that he lived a whole lifetime in a moment.

There was no flash of light, no realization. It was only the subtle comings on of nature. There was no fear. Illuminated, he felt emanate the vibrating guitar underneath his arm and before his chest; the sun vibrated in unison—had he heard it?—harmonious. Fire was procured; and ancient he grew. He would be the Earth. All stayed the same except perception. He would look into the rising sun, at dawn, and see the past, the future, thrumming with energy; beneath the sun, in that space between the risen sun and the Earth, floated bygone spirits of past practitioners who cooed, who made the impossible possible, who made visible the past, who solidified it, who vibrated it, who, cracking the seal that made people rational, made them imagine and sing.

On Death

He saw the snow. It was pure white before him, dense and serene. Snowflakes descended and fell onto the tree branches and the ground. All was white. He saw the snow, and it looked beautiful. Inside, Francis would be preparing coffee. The winter was cold, and Jimmy and he were outside chopping wood for a fire. He felt warm, the ersatz coolness of the evening nondescript outside of his thick gloves and heavy jacket. He heard the sound of the wood splintering and breaking. Jimmy had just turned eleven and was strong; he was a young man. Jimmy was tall for his age, five-eight Thomas would have guessed, and he had dark hair like his mother. He heard another splintering log. Thomas was watching over his son, an angel in the twilight. No matter how blue it got during this time the snow stayed white, whiter than anything Thomas had ever seen. It was beautiful, the twisting snowflakes in the breeze, the sugar-coated branches of trees, the crispness of the snow underfoot. It was all synchronized with his heart, and he loved it very much. Thomas loved his home, his son, his wife. He loved them very much. His son's red cheeks stuck out in the dim lighting. This told him it was time to go inside. Thomas and Jimmy took the chopped wood into their arms and brought it into the house.

The house was cool, but not cold. A fire would warm it up. On the window frames snow accumulated and made a pleasant looking coat. Thomas loved the winter. Thomas loved the winter like he loved his home. It was a time of pleasure, warmth, and Thomas relished the evenings when a fire was ablaze in the fireplace and a hot cup of coffee was between his hands and his son was sitting before the fire in his pajamas and his wife beside him was reading a book. It was all very marvelous.

"Jimbo," he called. His son turned around and faced him. Jimmy turned around and was no longer looking at the fire. "Jimbo," Thomas called.

Thomas woke with suddenness. He felt the air of the hospital enter his lungs. Jimbo was no longer there. Francis, as well, was gone. The fire blazing in the fireplace was replaced by a television. The family, winter was gone. Thomas was back in the hospital and the air of the hospital had just entered his lungs too quick—a gasp—and Thomas had awoken.

He had been having more dreams. Nostalgic images of years passed, and he knew he was close.

It was his kidneys. His body had rejected the donor kidney and, now, he was lying on his deathbed. The room was dark and chilling. Thomas pulled the blanket under his chin, studied the ceiling, and let out a deep breath. Yes, he had been dreaming.

Going to sleep was something he looked forward to. While in this hospital, it seemed, the old was displacing the new. It was as if a fissure had opened in his chest and all those old winter evenings came rushing in, like a door had just been opened. Thomas liked that. It comforted his sick body and aging mind. He closed his eyes and hoped to sleep. That was all he wanted; he wanted to fall back into his fantasies. He wanted to revisit his past and hold his wife and warm his bones by the fire with his son. They were satisfying, the dreams. They ended, abrupt; he would call his son each and every time. Jimbo would turn toward him and Thomas would wake up in a gasp. The air of the hospital entered his lungs the same way every time. Warm and white, he would wake and call his son again, in the hospital bed this time. Jimbo never spoke a word.

Thomas lay awake in the hospital bed for a hour or so before fading off into another sleep spell. This time he saw Jimbo chopping wood, this time Thomas felt cold, far too cold for comfort, and those thick gloves and that heavy coat were gone. Far too cold Thomas felt, and he watched on as Jimbo chopped wood, just kept chopping wood. He felt witless, helpless. Paralyzed, Thomas wanted to help chop that wood. He wanted to get involved. He wanted to touch Jimbo. He wanted to get inside and have coffee by the fire and watch his son in trance by the fire. Thomas was paralyzed. Perhaps it was fear. Perhaps it was the rashness of his attitude. He could not control himself and take the ax and chop wood. He watched and watched.

Then, again, he would call Jimmy. "Jimbo," he called. "Jimbo." Then, gasp, and he would wake up. This happened every time.

Once, Thomas dreamt of their trip to Miami and

water-skiing. Jimmy was there and he had on his father's sunglasses and looked like a real bachelor. This was when Jimmy was eight. He wore bright orange. His bathing suit was bright orange and stuck to his legs, as if he had just gotten out of the ocean. He wore the sunglasses. Man, did he look like a bachelor. He was handsome in the face, even at that age. His nose was wide, like his father's, and his lips were thick.

Looks like now you're the man, Thomas thought.

He woke with suddenness.

The sunrise was starting to peek over the horizon. It was morning. Thomas opened his eyes to slits and saw the nurse beside his bed checking his vitals and looking pretty in her scrubs. Thomas thought if she had children. The nurse had on extra weight around her abdomen and buttocks. Thomas noticed she held her weight well. It was a overall layer of fat, not accumulated in one spot. Thomas liked her. Thomas opened his eyes in full.

He said, "Good morning."

She said, "Good morning, Mr. Orville. How are you feeling?"

He said, "Not too bad. Say, could I have some water?"

"Sure, Mr. Orville," said the nurse, and she took a thermos from the bedside table and put some water in a plastic cup for Thomas. "Here you go," she said.

Thomas Orville swallowed in a dry throat. His throat hurt. He said, "Thank you."

Thomas Orville thought the family name was near an end. Orville. He was the last of them. The end of an era, as the say, he thought.

Jimbo was a long time gone now. It was Leukemia that took his son. Leukemia. It had come with ferocity. It took six months for the boy to die. Six months was all it took. Then, Thomas was alone. Jimmy was all Thomas had at that point, Francis having died of pneumonia a year prior. Jimmy was sixteen. Sixteen years was all Jimmy Orville had to live. Thomas thought, if he had known Jimmy was going to die, would he have lived any different, as a father, as a friend? Even then, he did not take well to fate.

At fifty-six years old, Thomas Orville started dreaming of his son. He had lived to see two millennia. So had his son. There was something rare in the fact, so rare that Thomas Orville closed his eyes and started crying. At fifty-six years old, Thomas Orville was dreaming of his son. One had much time to philosophize on their death bed. Thomas toyed with the concept of reincarnation. He thought his son had not. He thought for his son it was very simple. Thomas, now, did not feel simple. He felt complicated, more complicated than he had felt at any point in his entire life.

Thomas Orville was quite reluctant to die.

Apollo's

In the room furthest back from the front door was the grill. Eggs, bacon, Philly cheese steak, all kinds of breakfasts, were made in the back most room.

Apollo was yelling to his wife, Bethany, "Beth, can you get me my pack of cigarettes? They're in the drawer, underneath the cash register."

She was taking an order and did not respond.

"Beth! Cigarettes!"

Bethany shot a glance over her right shoulder, toward the back room, and turned back to the customers. "That will be right out," she said. She went behind the counter and got Apollo's cigarettes. "You are lucky if you get your cigarettes talking to me like that," she said. "I'm your wife, not your servant."

Apollo was flipping pancakes and did not respond.

Brusque, she thrusted the cigarettes into his arms, and they dropped to the floor.

"Beth, what the Hell? Are you acting up? Are you having another episode?"

"You're the one going through an episode, 'Pollo."

Again, he did not respond, but business was coming in torrents, and Apollo liked that. He could hear the bell above the door ringing when somebody walked in or out. It sounded like money. And he could hear the Bing! of the cash register opening and closing, the sounds of men and women talking and laughing, his wife chiding with the help they had on—a small Greek man, by the name of Arthur—and he heard the sizzling, the sizzling of many a breakfast before him, he the King of Apollo's, the most important man in the diner. Every customer would agree.

If they only knew what kind of life he lead out of the diner. They would be impressed, he thought, if they knew everything he had gone through to cook them breakfast and make this meager living.

Waking at four A.M. never fazed Apollo Diokos. Rising to take a shower at that time was close to a calling from Angels. Rinsing off sleep, rubbing shampoo into a lather. He was tall, well-groomed, and looked from the side like a hawk. His ardor was much like a hawk's, but in Brooklyn, New York, hawks were seen, infrequent, and men tended to look similar and skies were grayish most days out of the year, which was coy and reflective, Apollo thought, of the Brooklyn sidewalks and even, as years started to become longer, Apollo's mindset. If it were not for the wife, he thought, he would have been dead a long time ago. He would not have been so successful, owning his own diner on Seventeenth Street.

He woke on his own, this morning, the morning of May 12th, 2001, and went to the bathroom to brush his teeth, look into the mirror and notice once more that he was aging, to take a morning piss, and take a quick shower.

She was still in bed, but would get up in less than thirty

minutes, accompany him to work. She was the waitress, he the cook. They got on at five A.M., opened up, prepared food, tables, and unlocked the door for guests at six o'clock A.M.

Now, it was eleven. And people were starting to come in with more gusto. The rush was hitting and it would not slow until about two in the afternoon. It was Apollo's favorite time of the day. The hours passed with quickness, the coming and going of order slips and food never ceased and proceeded with smoothness, the jingle of the overhead bell never coming to an end.

It would all start with the preparation, and then, by eleven o'clock, it was like Grand Central Station. The phone would ring, the police department or the school district or another charity looking for a handout. The procession was unlike anything Apollo had ever seen. Taking everything for granted. Leaving nothing unturned. Speaking little, but in bursts that were important and graceful. These were the days of Apollo's diner, which lived in glory In other words, Apollo could not be happier than in those hours between eleven and two, when time seemed to speed up and customers came and went and Bethany, in her apron and curls, when he did catch a glimpse of her, looked beautiful, young and virile. She was a catch and he would not have been half the man he was that day if it were not for Bethany.

Each day she was anew. At night, she would put her hair in her curlers and, maybe, file her nails, brew tea, or bake a little something for Apollo and their little girl. In fact, she was more pretty than beautiful. It was a mysterious middle ground, where beauty was left up to the imagination and all that was with surety present was her prettiness—her uniform brown eyes and hair.

Apollo was brought out of his daze when his wife called to him that a customer's eggs were to be made sunny side up instead of over easy.

"Got it," he said. He sucked on cigarettes the entire time throughout the workday. It was a wonder he could still breathe at thirty-five. Twenty years he had been smoking. It started back in his hometown and he had not stopped. It helped him think, he one day realized. On that day, he made the decision never to quit smoking.

He had heard of an American saying. What was it? Something about dying young and living to the fullest. He was not able to recall with clarity, but what did it matter. On a day like this, when everybody wanted their full of corn beef hash and hash browns, what did it matter?

Two o'clock he relaxed.

"Is it time to do the count?" asked Bethany.

"Do the count," said Apollo.

Bethany opened the cash register and took the money out and laid it on the counter top. It was time for Arthur to go, and he got paid cash every day. They picked him up three years back, and he was a good addition to the diner, pulling his weight and doing chores without being asked.

"How are you feeling?" Apollo asked, while Bethany was counting the morning's earnings.

"How am I feeling? I'm well, 'Pollo," she said, and left it at that.

"Did I upset you badly earlier?" Apollo asked.

"Not more than usual. I swear, it's like you're a different person in that room."

"It's work, Beth, you have to know that. I have my mind set in work mode. It's nothing personal."

"Well, I take it personally sometimes," she said. "You don't have to make such strong demands."

"I'll keep that in mind."

Arthur was taking care of the few patrons in the dining room as Bethany was counting the money.

"We made about two hundred and fifty dollars," she said. "Not bad for half a day's work."

"We can do better," Apollo said. "Arthur, take your money and go! And have a good day. You did well today.

Arthur said, "Thanks, Apollo," collected his money, and exited the building.

"Another three hours, then the dinner rush starts," said Apollo, looking at his wife and smiling.

"Yes, Apollo. I'm looking forward to it."

He said, "I love you."

She said, "I love you, too," but she did not mean it.

At home, the family was readying for bed, when the little girl, Susan, said, "Daddy, I don't want to go to bed just yet." The family was in the living area, watching television when the girl said this. "I don't want to go to bed, Daddy. Show me how to play the piano."

There was a piano in the dining room, which Apollo had not played in years. He used to play for the girl when she was young, a baby; and Susan had even told her father that her earliest memory was of him playing the piano in her second year.

He had been taken aback by the comment. She had a good memory, he thought. Two years old and having consciousness. Not too bad.

Apollo said to the girl, "I can't now, but tomorrow maybe."

To which the girl said, "Daddy, you never spend time with me. What if you get hit by a car tomorrow and we can't play piano?"

"That wouldn't happen."

"But, what if."

Apollo took the girl into his arms and brought her to her bedroom. There, he tucked her into bed. "Tomorrow," he said, "we'll play the piano. I promise."

She nodded and turned on her side.

Back in the living area, Bethany was watching the news, and said without turning her head, "You should have played the piano for her."

"Why?" he asked.

"Because you don't spend enough time with her. We're bad parents, really."

"We're not bad parents."

"'Pollo, we are. She's in school, then she comes home and is alone for the better part of the day. That's no way to raise a child."

"We're not bad parents."

"Pollo, we are."

"You know what," he said. "I've had enough of your cynicism."

"What cynicism? I'm just being factual."

"Factual or un-factual, it's cynicism." That was enough, he thought. He would let her speak and would say nothing in return.

Only she said nothing. He had gotten the last word in, which made him look like a smart ass. It was exactly what he did not want. But she had shut up too soon.

Why make her out to be so bad, though, he thought. Was she that bad? Sure, sometimes she had her opinions, which were off putting, but was she so bad?

He thought, yes. Why not? He doubted she ever doubted herself, as he did only too often. Maybe confidence was what he was lacking of late. Maybe that was why getting up in the morning was getting so hard, cooking for all those people so hellish.

"I'm sorry," he said.

"No, you're not," she said.

"I am," he said. "And I'll prove it to you. Only not today. Not now, but someday, somewhere." He noticed this came off as a bit sarcastic. "I'm not lying," he said.

"You're not," she said. "Have you ever?"

He did not know how to respond to that. It was a loaded question. It must have been. "No," he said, quite aware that that was a lie.

"Good! Don't," she said, and left it at that. She was sipping on her tea for many moments before she said, "I'm going to bed. And I'm turning the heat on."

Apollo said, "Don't turn the heat on."

"Fine," she said.

He said, "We can share body heat."

"You would like that."

"Why not?" he said.

"Because I'm a cold bitch."

"Fine," he said, and he left it at that.

The next day was a Sunday, and Apollo's would be closed. Every week, the family went, on Sunday, to church. Passing by the large, ornate building every so often, when it was not a Sunday, and doing a cross, left Apollo questioning his faith, and it seemed, after a while, that faith no longer held any substantiality. It was only the facts. Only the facts mattered—Beth's work ethic, how Susan was doing in school, how the diner was doing—so much so that when Sunday came around Apollo went to church only to cover up the fact that he was losing faith.

On the way to church, and in his best suit, Apollo turned to Bethany and asked, with a face serene and calm, "Beth, am I dominant?"

"What kind of question is that," was the response.

"Am I dominant? I just want to know what you think."

"'Pollo," she said. "It's not a matter of being dominant. You're a great man."

"So, the answer is no," he said.

"The answer is not no," said Bethany. "Sometimes you are headstrong, and you don't make the right decisions, but you're not too headstrong, and you make good decisions at times." She laughed and turned her face towards him. "Where is this coming from?"

"Pay me no mind," he said. "I'm a rat."

"No, you're not."

"No you're not, Daddy," said Susan from the backseat.

Apollo was silent, pulled into a spot along shore road, and got out of the small Chevrolet, opened the door for Susan. "I appreciate it."

Bethany was dressed in one of her black dresses, the kind that made Apollo think of death and other morbid topics. She had worn that dress in particular when her Uncle died, back in '97. It was tragic. He had died in a car accident and was burned in the face. The funeral was a closed casket funeral.

"You look lovely," Apollo said.

"As do you," she said. And then she kissed him on his mouth. It felt like a kiss from a dark woman, some woman who killed her late husband to take all his money. But, he knew this was nothing more than paranoia. He loved her. But, he started doubting the foundation of his love for her—that is that nothing can and will go wrong, that nothing while with a strong woman can take a turn for the worse. It was a wives' tale, that strong men had strong women backing them. In many cases, the woman was there for the money and nothing more. It was lucky this was not the case as far as Apollo was concerned. She had taught him a bit of respectability. And he cherished that in her. But, when things got hot and she went into one of her episodes, he felt like drowning the broad. Stop that, he thought, as he walked up the front stairs to the church. She's a fine woman, and she's helped me out in my life. I would still be drinking too much whiskey and driving around all night if it wasn't for her. I should be thanking her.

He held the door open for Bethany and Susan.

"Thank you," Bethany said.

"Thank you," Susan said.

They could hear the monk-like, ritualized singing from the inside of that church, and it filled him with awe and the fear of God. It was something like looking over a cliff, into a canyon. One had nothing to support themselves and just how far down it was nobody knew and there was very little to gain perspective.

He had gone to the Grand Canyon once with his Aunts and Uncles, before he met Bethany. It was a miraculous experience. It was not so much mystical as it was enlightening, that something so serene could be so large.

It was a huge excavation of nature's own. Just what nature was searching for nobody knew. Peace? Ideas? Hope? It was reminiscent of Apollo's own personal excavations of the soul, and like the gray clouds overhead and the gray sidewalks beneath his feet, here in Brooklyn, symbolized his state of mind of late, the blue skies and tawny cliff sides symbolized his state of mind in his youth. He would never forget the trip out West, where the sun set reddish-gold and the expanse just outside of Las Vegas bordered on the realm of holy and the Bonneville Salt Flats were nothing more than a boy's dream, clinging to something real as the Earth, because that was what it was, Earth, material; and now, as Apollo did his cross, standing opposite the priest on this Sunday in St. John's Greek Orthodox church, Apollo felt scared, scared of death, scared of life, scared of everything that moved, and sung, and danced, scared of ghosts and spirit, scared of God—or what he symbolized anyway.

Apollo knew that communion was like a nail in the coffin. There was still time to back out, to be a coward, never acknowledge God again, and go through life as an atheist. Beth would not have it, though. And when the priest called up the rows and rows of Greek denizens, Apollo swallowed knowing that the wine and bread was only a symbol, that God existed in the recesses of the human imagination, and in children, and in the piano. Apollo knew that God was standing beside him—he was his family—and often times, he looked down on them, was disgusted even, in their mannerisms. But, why, he thought, not? It was the twenty-first century, and people had in them a streak of cynicism, and maybe even fear.

Apollo wondered if fear stained the soul, what color it would be, if the soul existed, and how much it could put up with. He thought it could put up with quite a bit. But, even then, as the liturgy came to a close, Apollo felt somewhere between his calmness and serenity a bit of impatience. Apollo felt he wanted to go home and see what he could remember on the piano—it had been so many years. And most of all Apollo wanted to get back to the diner and fry up a pair of eggs and a couple slices of bacon, in his diner, where he was of importance.

Of Interest

Half past six, Evert and Linda Jameson were sitting in their favorite café, the table a blue and white plaid tablecloth, with candles flickering, the floor waxed and made of hard wood. A barista was attending two patrons who had entered and sat down to a table nearby the Jameson's. Evert and Linda were sitting, patient and waiting for their chai tea, the café the type of place where Evert did not mind waiting, for every time he went into this café he saw something different, so many things were on the walls. Bright red tricycles hanging by ropes, hay brooms stuck to racks, chessboards, too, hanging from the ceiling by fishing line.

"We could go there and pick him up," Linda was saying. She was twenty-five years old and Evert was twenty-six. "We could go there and pick him up. We'd only be gone a week at most." The barista came over with their chai and she set the tea in front of them, and returned to her station behind the counter.

Evert Jameson took a sip of his chai, then said, "You know I'm not against it, but can't we choose a better time?"

"A better time?" said Linda. "This is the best time, the only time. He's waiting for us in Nairobi."

Nairobi, Evert thought, rather put off by her words,

which seemed impulsive, but he had patience with her the three years they had been together, and he loved her very much. "I don't think I can fit it into my schedule," he said.

"You can! I know you can!" said Linda. "Oh, how I love black babies. They're so cute in the face and their smooth, creamy skin is so beautiful. Oh, how I love black babies."

Evert shot a glance to the corner of the café, an African-American man, who was tending his own chai. Evert felt embarrassed. The African-American man, though, did not seem to hear her. "I'm not against it," he said. "But can't we choose a better time?"

"A better time?" said Linda. "This is the best time."

"I don't think I can fit it into my schedule," he said.

"You're against this!" Linda said.

"I am not."

"You're against this!" Linda said.

"Don't make a scene, Linda," Evert said.

"I'm not making a scene," Linda said. "But, I just figured—you're against this."

See if I take you out again, he thought. Quiet and reserved, Evert Jameson was the type of man who, for a long while, thought she was getting verbose. Of late, she would speak outright nonsense, childish, with a substantial dose of naïvety.

"Oh, Evert, it would be magical," she said. "Don't you know the wonder in such charity?"

"I know," he said. "But can't we choose a better time?"

"A better time?" Linda said. "This is the best time. Oh,

Evert, it would be so interesting!"

"I'm interesting," Evert said. "It's hard to believe how interesting I am. It's hard to believe." He sat, meditative. "Can't we just conceive our own," he said.

"We could," she said. "But where's the charity in that?"

"I don't know. It's charitable as it is, having children. Why do you need one now? What brought this on? Have you been talking to Lisa again?"

"That liberal? No, I haven't been," she said, but he didn't believe her.

"I've just been thinking to myself, late at night, when you're asleep, how nice it would be to have a child, a baby, in the house."

Feeling betrayed, in the sense that she thought about such things as he slept beside her, Evert took another drink of his chai. "I don't think I can fit it into my schedule," he said.

"You can, Evert. Don't lie to me. I know you're against this. Are you against this?"

"You know, the more you carp about it, the more I feel inclined to say yes I am against this."

"I knew it. You'd be a great father, Evert, a great father. The obvious differences, he being from Africa, would go unnoticed after a few months. You'd be a great father, Evert, a great father."

Evert felt he needed a glass of chardonnay, hearing her talk like this, but did not order one, and let slip away her remarks, virility obsolete, Evert Jameson a withering flower, the rudiments of angst permeating in his psyche, taking a last sip of chai, and setting down the paper cup on the table. He looked at his wife, who, opaque, sat between fabricated endearment and his would-be masculinity, and separated the couple in a fine and opalescent tear, pressuring him, a catastrophic imminence in his gut, telling him he was, in fact, uncharitable, that she was, and that they were to be parents, not of their own, but that of a foreign birthright. It absconded his usual good temper, and made brusque his smoothness, rendering arid his sweetness. He said, "What would it take?"

She said, "Like anything worthwhile, it takes determination."

"And luck," he said.

"Luck plays a part. But that's where you come in."

"How so?" he asked.

"You, as a parent, keep luck at bounds, and fate, too. You're the mediator."

Evert flushed at the thought. He felt not empowered, nor did he feel a father; he felt childish and silly. The flight, the child, the paperwork, the city, Nairobi, the trip home, the homecoming, their first dinner as a family. It was all very impractical. It was all very confining. The taking in of a boy removed him from reality. His head started spinning. His heart started throbbing, and, quite sudden. he felt his brow start to perspire. Incandescent rays of light hit the tables and walls and people around him with vigor, an imperceptive itch on his back taking prescience, his head gray.

"Oh, it would be so interesting," she said, at last.

"I love you," he said.

"I love you, too," she said.

"But, I just can't do it," he said.

A few seconds passed, and she said, "Fine. If you loved me you would do it."

"Don't say that," he said. "I love you. I really love you."

Linda, flustered, got up from the table. She traversed the floor to the restroom. Evert sat alone and he thought if he had made the right choice. It was not the right time. They were young. It, with definitiveness, was not the right time. She returned, and she looked as if she had been crying. "Are you ready to go?" she asked.

"Yes," he said.

The arose together and exited the café. Outside, the stars shone like gems in slate rock. The Floridian atmosphere clung to their necks. Evert had cooled off. Linda sniffled and shook her head. The car was just around the bend. The sky, as they drove westward, toward their home, was being sucked in a backward direction, toward the café and toward the beach. The night was receding.

"I hope I didn't ruin your night," he said.

"You didn't," she said, thinking he ruined her life. "It's just that I thought you'd be all for it."

"I'm not against it, but can't we choose a better time?"

"Oh, Evert," she said, not looking at him. She looked out the window. "Oh, Evert."

In Columbus

Timmy always wore this necklace. It had a blue gem set in a brass ring and made you notice his blue eyes with more intensity. He never took it off and it became sort of a mystery where it had gone. He claims he outgrew it, tossed it in the lake behind his house, but everybody thought he had begun to believe it made him looked less masculine and did away with it for that reason and for that reason alone. The teenager started to notice girls' curvaceousness and began to notice more so the bulge in his pants which was becoming more like his father's. He was the tallest out of his group of friends at the time and that made him feel like he was supposed to be the leader, and he did lead friends out to the diner where they got root beer floats and to the movies where they watched movies like *Nightmare on Elm Street* and *Indiana Jones and the Last Crusade*. He looked up to Harrison Ford's Dr. Jones, but he did not that tell to anybody.

Sitting around the table, drinking soda, they talked about school, basketball. They were young then, and nothing really mattered. Only the baby blue skies that spread like a coverlet above them and, at night, the silver dollar moon which casted downward its sublime rays.

Timmy was saying something about Antarctica. Everything, from witches to the color spectrum, enthralled them and they possessed a precocious hunger which would at some point become pertinent nostalgia—a lull in the conversation—and they poked fun at Lester the parakeet who was beside the table, caged and lithe, and then Timmy's momma came rushing out saying the cat was giving birth, and they all got up, sodas in hand, and went into the garage where little Fanny was mewing away and stretching her legs and breathing with rapidity, and they sat in a circle.

Sure, girls were into him and he was getting into them. He even thought about having babies. He was too young, he knew, to be thinking that, but nobody ever knew what went on in that head with its corporeal side-swept hair and black eyebrows. He even kissed a girl by the bleachers and there was tongue. He liked it, and he knew she did, too, but they never did it again.

Whiskey was the first drink they shared. Burning their throats and mouths, one boy doubling over and expelling the swig from his nostrils, they finished half the bottle and put it back in Timmy's father's liquor cabinet. It stayed there until freshman year of high school when there was a Sadie Hawkins dance, and Louise Rhodes asked Timmy to be her date. He accepted and he wore a blue suit to match her blue dress. The suit was off blue and did not match Louise's dress, but that was okay. Nobody seemed to notice.

1990 came and went and youth turned out to be a sham and Timmy was moving into a heady state of alertness, brought about by an increased wariness in fashion and his learning to play the guitar. The guitar was a 1982 Martin acoustic and sounded quite good. Crisp chords, shapely chord changes impressed just about everyone who heard him play. That rather ended with abruptness. Timmy dislocated a finger playing basketball, and that was that—his finger kept locking up—and the Martin grew dusty, older, in the corner of his brown room.

The little one, whose mew sounded like a squeaker, did not make it; the majority of them thought it a blessing that the little one was in a better place—he was small and pathetic and he did not have a chance. The other cats soaked up that energy in the womb, leaving nothing for Squeaker. Survival of the fittest. That seemed to be the theme of late.

Cucumbers, tomatoes, onions, parsley, and oregano. In those types of crops were where Timmy's father invested most of his time. He would water, weed, and seed his garden every season and would harvest them in time for autumn. The fruits were large and bright and tasty, and the spices had more of a zing compared to the store bought spices, and Timmy liked that. During the summer, Timmy would get a glass of soda and sit on the teak wood furniture out back and daydream. Timmy's father would be in the garden, but Timmy seldom helped him out.

Sunday morning, Timmy got punched in the nose. He was talking about Fanny giving birth, and the little one who did not make it, and said he liked it better that way. Reid, who was always a nut, broke an o-ring and got all red in the face, called Timmy a fucker, and tagged him. Timmy's nose was bleeding pretty bad, but that was not the first time there was blood that weekend, the cat having bled thirty-six hours prior a maroon fluid that seemed to be only half blood. The nurse fixed him up and sent him home. She said she thought it was broken. It was crooked and it would never get straightened out in full. But, they were young then, and nothing really matters.

The Beauty in Bereavement

Judy Tremont stroked her dying husband's hair. Augustus had been sick for nearing five years and now the end was near. His gray hair, combed by Judy's long, manicured fingernails which were feathery and light, had the ambience of a man wishing to depart his shell.

Days and nights, Augustus while semi-unconscious tossed in a rapture that could only be the dance of a dying man; for, as Judy Tremont watched her husband lingering on the cusp of death, she heard the whispering of the vast plane which claimed the departed, and she feared it and loathed it. She thought if Augustus knew how close he was to death, which was to her so near that it sent shivers up her spine and put goosebumps on her skin. She thought not; no, he did not know, this poor man, this collection of flesh, how close he was to the everlasting.

She stoked his hair and cooed him. He turned over by the will of a weightless spirit, his eyes open and moist, and told her in a voice frail and final that he loved her. Augustus Tremont died, his eyes closed, and his breath let out, moist and thick onto Judy's face. Judy could hear the tea kettle singing. She was making tea for herself and would try to have Augustus drink a little. But, he was gone; the tea kettle whistled and she went downstairs, leaving her departed husband on his deathbed, went into the kitchen, and poured herself a cup of chamomile. The sweet chamomile filled her sinuses and pores. She would have to call someone—the hospital, the morgue. But, that could wait. Now, she wanted to drink chamomile and sit and think for a while before she went upstairs and stoked Augustus's hair some more, cried, and remembered Halifax and St. Augustine.

Those were her brightest and most vivid memories of Augustus, and they were the memories by which she wished to remember him. Not in this state of sickness.

The linoleum floor was cold under her feet and the floral wallpaper—red roses and eucalyptus—was ambient and serene. Outside, snow was falling, white and pleasant. She found herself finishing her cup of chamomile, set the cup in the sink to be washed, and went upstairs to Augustus's side, the hardwood flooring creaking, the house settling, and then she sat on the edge of the bed and sang:

The road is open, for the men
who walk alone, but for a time
with them are the songs of tragedienne.

The blood had run from Augustus's face and his face was pale and peaceful. Her song went unheard. She could not even hear the words; it was as if her voice were a ways away.

She lay down in bed and went to sleep. A vague presence then filled her senses. She knew she was asleep, but she could distinguish a person in the room. The person walked from the doorway to Augustus's side and it seemed—no, it felt—as if the man took something from Augustus's front pajama pocket and deposited it in the man's own. The sallow apparition continued out of the room, descended the staircase, went into the kitchen, and by some form of sentience Judy knew he had a cup of chamomile and disappeared, vanished into the ethereal substance from which he came.

Judy's eyes opened and it was night. The snow continued to fall and was accumulating on the window sill. Before long she closed her eyes and fell into a sound sleep.

She studied the inside of her closed eyelids. While sleeping, she became conscious and felt Augustus's body warm beside hers. He was lying on his back. Dreaming but aware, she thought of the sallow man, Augustus, and the morning, and she felt Augustus's body become light and cool, and then felt it rise up and exit through the window; she thought the room smelled of firewood. She awoke to the light of day, turned over, and noticed that Augustus's body was still there. She would have to make a phone call.

Downstairs, the chamomile tasted good, the room spacious.

Judy Tremont made two phone calls that morning, the first to her friend Betty Silverman and the second to Bethesda Hospital North. She sat in the kitchen waiting for her friend to arrive and though the lingering presence she had felt the night before was still in her memory, she knew it was only a thought, a hallucination. What more could it be? An angel? By God, did she believe in the supernatural? She thought she better start believing if she wanted to see her beloved again and she poured another cup of chamomile. This was her third cup this morning. It was nearing ten A.M.

The doorbell rang, Judy went to the front door, and opened it. Betty Silverman stood there with a bouquet of roses in her hand and her pocketbook on her shoulder. Snow was falling and clung to her shoulders and hair.

"Come in," said Judy.

"Bless you, Judy, bless you. If this isn't a day for blessings, I don't know what is."

"Chamomile?"

"Please."

She poured a cup of tea for her lifelong friend and contemplated telling her of the dreams she had had. She somehow felt compelled to keep it a secret, as if those types of dreams were meant for the dreamer and the dreamer alone, but she knew she would tell Betty because she was a friend and a good friend at that.

"It happened yesterday evening," said Judy.

"A tragedy, but life is the obstacle, not death."

Judy wished she agreed. It seemed somehow selfish of her to think that she was robbed of Augustus, that he deserved more time on Earth, but who was she? A woman, simple, plain, and a widow.

"You have the best tea, Judy, I assure you. The best tea."

Judy got her tea from the same apothecary her whole life. A small place downtown that was an emporium of herbs and holistic, natural medicine, which for the life of her Judy had no idea how to administer. It was captivating—the jars of herbs like sarsaparilla, dried rose buds, and valerian root. But, she stuck with her chamomile not just because it tasted good, but because it was the only herb she knew anything about in the whole store. Walking into Mary's Apothecary, one was taken by the subtle scents of herbs, which to Judy seemed a sort of mystical occurrence, the olfactory particles and motes of light absorbed in the furtive ambience, the collected botanics.

Judy took a sip of her chamomile, which was still hot. A sense of recalcitrance went through her. She had invited Betty, but something was far too ordinary about the scenario, as if this Sunday morning were a day straight out of a cache of normality. It was far from normal. Augustus was dead and there was nothing she could do about it.

Betty Silverman was saying something, but Judy did not hear her and spoke sharp and loud so that Betty would cease her attempts and provocations of closure and philosophy, and said, "I had a dream."

"A dream?" said Betty Silverman. "A good dream or a bad dream?"

Judy said, "I don't know, but a dream."

"Well? Do tell."

Judy looked into her teacup and saw filaments of chamomile floating in the yellow liquid. "I was lying in bed next to Augustus and it felt as though somebody came into the room and took something out of his pocket, went downstairs, had a cup of tea, and then was gone. I felt Augustus's body rise and exit the bedroom window and that was it."

"Dear God. You poor thing."

"It was homely and nice and I didn't feel afraid. I woke up, had a cup of tea, and called you. And then I called Bethesda Hospital North."

"Dear God. You poor thing."

"And then you arrived in what seemed sixty seconds later."

"Dear God." Betty Silverman gaped at Judy and Judy could tell she was trying to think of something to say but nothing would come up.

Judy finished her chamomile, got up from the kitchen table, and set the cup in the sink.

"I'd say it's a miracle, an angel. He's in heaven. He must be."

"He was a good man."

"You poor thing."

Judy felt patronized. Perhaps a lifetime of being alone and sleeping with men half your age, a tendency of Betty Silverman, came with its egotism. Judy Tremont did not judge her friend—she never had—but something in the way she said it, "You poor thing," made Judy's heart skip, as if the departed were trying to communicate. Maybe it was a good thing to have Betty here, she thought. She keeps me company until Bethesda Hospital North gets here and then she will leave and I will take a bath, a cool bath to cleanse myself. I will go for a walk in the evening through the snow and feel Augustus beside me as if we were in our twenties again, and then I'll come home, have tea, and relax, and then I'll go to sleep and imagine Augustus was there with me.

The doorbell rang.

"It must be Bethesda Hospital North," Judy said, and it was.

"Where is the corpse?" asked a young man in blue scrubs.

"Augustus is upstairs in his bed," said Judy, and she noted the sarcasm. It would take an oracular someone to get through to the youth of this age, she thought, and led them up the stairs, which creaked and groaned. Judy opened the white wooden door and she saw Augustus, peaceful in bed where she had left him. "There he is," she said. "Be careful with him."

"We will, miss," said the other of the two. "You don't have to stay here and watch. We'll be quick and we won't touch anything." The bigger of the two men opened up the stretcher and said, "One, two," and on three they picked up Augustus, whose head lolled to the side and Judy thought he looked heavy, old, and quite lifeless. His sumptuous head was leaving this house for the last time and she would never stroke his hair again in the same way, in the way she had stoked it twelve hours ago, when he said his final words to her, subtle, airy, and warm. The two men heaved Augustus Tremont down the stairs. Judy watched the ambulance drive away through the snow. She went back into the kitchen to find Betty Silverman waiting at the kitchen table. The cups had been washed and put away and Betty seemed eager to speak but said nothing. Judy sensed Betty's trying to use her seeming and innate ableness to enliven the moment as if it were one of her beaus but Betty did not say anything and nodded.

"If you are so inclined," Judy said, "would you like to go for a walk?"

"It's snowing," Betty said, "but sure. I think a walk would be good about now."

Judy dressed according to the weather—a heavy coat, red scarf, and earmuffs Augustus had bought her for her birthday years ago—and they went outside into what was becoming a clear afternoon. I'm going to need to reorder my life, Judy thought, thinking Augustus was her center and that her life was for him. Restart with an ubiquitous happiness that no death can collapse. The wind blew the snowfall into a frenzy and it was too cold to go for a walk, but what else was there to do? The house was empty, quiet, as if disorder had been vaporized and an uncanny lightness took its place.

That was what death was, Judy reflected. A transposition of order and disorder, the Universe taking responsibility for its own actions, its own virile phenomenon. Virile, under her feet, the snow crunched, crisp, and Judy thought, God, how unearthly.

The only son of Judy Tremont lived in Chicago, Illinois. He received a call from work at four in the afternoon. It was the third phone call Judy Tremont made that day. "I'll be down tomorrow," Franklin Tremont said. "I'll catch the morning flight." He had not visited his home state of New York for over ten years and had not kept in close contact with his parents. He called only on birthdays and Christmas, but he loved his parents very much to the extent that any son would and they received his calls with open hearts and they were on good terms ever since he moved to the Windy City. Two wives and two kids later, Franklin Tremont was just starting to realize what his first and immediate family meant to him. It was too late. Too late to get to know his father, Augustus Tremont, on a more intimate level. The first reaction he had upon hearing of his father's death was guilt and remorse. He never believed in God. God was like a breeze that tousled his hair and went on to greater things, Franklin thought, and that was not to say he was not philosophical or thoughtful on the subject. Eighteen years of Sundays left a pretty real taste in his mouth regarding the Holy Trinity, the trifecta that was going to deliver his soul to Heaven and had delivered his father's not twenty-four hours ago.

Now, he drank wine in the evenings when he got home from work and over dinner prepared for him and his sons by his wife, Trish, but it did not signify the blood of Christ and the bread he ate was not His body, and when he closed his eyes at night thinking of tomorrow's coffee, breakfast, Trish and his two sons, one five years old, the other six, he fell into sleep so deep it was primordial.

Everlasting life was not a hopeful notion to Franklin as it was to many Catholics throughout the world, it was fact. Like a drop in a bucket, life and willpower oscillated out like ripples and became one with the greater entity that was the Universe. He did not converse on topics such as religion. A modest man, Franklin Tremont, was quiet and kept to himself and as he saw it power was in silence. An idea gained momentum and substantiality that way. It was physics and he knew he had the right idea. Iconoclast images from youth radiated through him, Father taking him fishing along the .

Hudson River, Father showing him how to throw a baseball, experiences idiosyncratic and youthful.

Now, a definite tear separated him and his father. Not just one, Franklin thought, but two. One: the scape between the living and the departed. And two: five hundred miles between Chicago, Illinois and upstate New York.

Boarding the 757, Delta flight 3019B, he was breaching the easier and more immediate of the two fissures. In about two hours, he would land in Laguardia Airport, rent a car, and drive north three hours to arrive in the small town of Carmel, New York.

Carmel reabsorbed him upon his arrival; it rekindled a lost childhood that was once so real to Franklin Tremont and it redefined him. The brisk air of Carmel was not like Chicago's. Here, you breathed and Carmel breathed back. It was a jovial reciprocity that tended toward the notion Franklin was having in recent months—take the kids out of Chicago. It was realistic, finding a job in the city, commuting the three hours from Carmel to New York and being closer to his parents; now, just one parent, his mother, who when she called seemed laconic and at the same time apprehensive.

Franklin Tremont pulled up to the familiar house, the house in which he grew up, and turned off the rental. He walked to the front door. His breath was visible. He breathed out fumes of warmth, steam. He knocked on the mahogany door. Judy Tremont opened it and did not smile. She did not waver nor did she look inviting. She looked sick.

Judy thought her son, thirty-five years old, looked in his heavy coat with the collar turned up ostentatious. Yes, she reflected, he looks like he's from Chicago; a city boy we seem to have raised.

"Hi, Ma."

Judy moved to the side and said, "Come in out of the cold. It's freezing and you're letting the heat out."

Franklin Tremont moved from the outdoors to the warmth of his childhood home. He took off his coat and hung it on the coat hanger.

"Glad to see you got here in one piece. How was the flight?"

"It was swell, Ma, swell."

"Would you like some tea?"

"Coffee?"

"Haven't any."

"Shucks."

"How long will you be staying?"

"I'll be leaving tomorrow afternoon."

"That's okay."

"How are you feeling?"

"Cold and brittle."

"It's good to be home," Franklin said. "The circumstances could be a little better."

"Come into the kitchen, Frank. Welcome home." Judy sat at the kitchen table. She had a cup of chamomile. "Augustus is gone," she said. "But, it was a long time coming. That was the worst of my problems, seeing him in that state. Now, all I have to worry about is my osteoporosis and my orthopedic wellbeing."

"Do you have pain?"

"Every day."

"Rats."

"Betty Silverman was here earlier when they took Augustus away. You remember Betty, don't you?"

He remembered her well. The feline eyes and straight teeth. He felt by her, however, a little put off, as if she had a sort of innate vanity. "I remember her. How is she?"

"Verbose, as usual."

"Typical. I remember the last time I saw Betty. God, it must be twenty years ago now. We went to a museum in the city. I forget which. She told me she was envious of Nefertiti."

"That sounds like Betty. She's always got an eye out for who's better or worse off."

"Like that one time she went down to Islamorada for Christmas and came back saying it was the worst time of her life. She liked a white Christmas and down there was only heat and greaseballs." He was trying to make his mother laugh. She was not biting. "In all actuality," he said, "we have it the best up here, where there are seasons. You like the seasons, don't you? The change?"

"Yes, sure, honey. I like the seasons." Judy was far off, thinking about the man she had married, the never-ending laughter and warmth, and thought of his body in the morgue with the other bodies, ichor and insects, and said, "You know, I was hoping he would outlast me. That sounds selfish, doesn't it? That I would go first."

"No, it isn't," Franklin said. "That's human." A serpentine shiver slithered up his spine. "Don't be ashamed. Some people around the world celebrate death, like the Mexicans."

"I don't want to hear about Mexicans," Judy said. She then let out an elephantine trumpet laugh and tears started coming from her eyes. "I remember when we got you that jacket for Christmas, the one with green stripes on it and how Augustus said it looked so girly."

"I remember that jacket," said Franklin. "Dad took it out of my closet when I was asleep and donated it to the Salvation Army. I liked that jacket."

Attentiveness exchanged places with melancholy in Judy's eyes. Franklin noticed color coming into her cheeks like she was blushing and was revitalized by the change. If it was one thing Franklin could not ascertain it was if his mother's life would better or worsen now that his father was gone. She took care of him five years throughout his sickness and yet avoided attrition.

"Everything is going to be all right," Franklin said.

"Oh, I know everything is going to be all right," Judy said. She sounded a bit absconding. "Oh, I've been so astute throughout this whole time and finally he's left me."

Franklin Tremont thought of fate. Some people wished the departed luck and went about their lives with glee. Some did not. Some clung to the departed and felt stark avarice all the while. "Do you still go to church?" Franklin asked.

Judy said, "No."

Franklin thought of his first girlfriend. She sang in the church choir; she was an alto and sang well. If it was one thing his mother needed it was sound, music, something to keep away the silence. "I'm going to get you a stereo system."

"A stereo system? I don't want one."

"It's going to be so quiet in here. You need something, some music, something. I'm going to get you a stereo system with six disk changer and you can listen to Edith Piaf, how does that sound? In 2016 Anno Domini."

"I don't know how to work a stereo system."

"It's easy. You don't even need an Allen wrench."

"Okay. Buy me a stereo system and I'll listen to Edith Piaf."

"That's more like it. Something to alleviate the silence."

The total stillness of night shook Judy Tremont with abrasiveness. Franklin was in his childhood bedroom. She could not get to sleep. The room was warm and she felt well but the silence and the empty spot beside her kept her cold. She lay on her back, her eyes closed. Judy saw images flash by in her mind's eye. The Statue of Liberty. Augustus, twenty-five years of age. It was eerie and noiseless.

Judy did not think of herself in all her seventy-six years of life as a victim. Now, the melodrama of victimization sifted into her like a winter chill. It was uncomfortable and she was uneasy. The friends of her youth still had their husbands save Rita Purcell, a childhood friend who lost her husband to massive stroke and never remarried. Judy remembered the incident well. She thought it would be quite simple for Rita. Rita Purcell was young then and could remarry. But, the postmortem depression was too much. She skulked and was not seen often henceforth. Judy Tremont feared the same would happen to her. She did not want to fall out of camaraderie. I should start attending church, she thought; and then dismissed the thought as desperate and sappy.

What travesty death was. It came and it went, coldhearted. It left nothing in return. The departed were the departed and that was that. The dark expanse before her eyes opened into exquisite fear, which was bordered by loneliness and apathy. She felt guilt and embraced it for the lack of Augustus's body and remembered a present Augustus had bought her for no reason at all, just because he loved her and wanted to see her smile—a tapestry with a green woodsy scene, a deer drinking from a stream. She could not remember why she did not like it. It was something from Augustus. She should have been happy and accepting, shown that she liked it when she did not. The tapestry hung above the mantle for two weeks before she took it down, rolled it up, and placed in the garage. Augustus never mentioned it. He must have thought it trivial, a bygone throe that his wife must have been experiencing regarding the tapestry. Women, he must have thought, and ten years later he would roll over in bed and breath in Judy's face his final words, a spiritual telecommunication between two aged and imperfect lovers.

Judy opened her eyes. The digital clock read 2:32 A.M. She was not tired. However, she was. She wanted the morning to come so she could have a reason to rise and drink tea. The Earth claimed everybody, downtrodden as was its nature. Time was the only factor, the when and where and how of death. Not the if. No, not the if, she thought. Not the if. Judy had a subtle but provoking grasp on death; she knew the material body was just that—

material—and that when it died the mind expanded into the realm of whatever inclination the individual had in store—intellect, creativity. She remembered her youth while lying in bed. How inferior she felt to the other girls before she started reading Plath and Shakespeare. That was her first awakening. Literature. And then, her second realization was that she was a stickler for "good boys." One night of Everclear with Ray Richards in 1945 was all she needed to figure that out. Augustus came along in 1950 and she knew she found a real man. She found, in youth, boys debilitating; and Augustus seemed to alleviate some pressure and the mystery of sex became a very real thing and she started standing, her back erect, with more confidence after meeting Augustus, a sense of pride in her bones, which now had grown frail and porous. Youth had been a noble venture, she reflected, it nearing now 3 A.M.

Insofar as reminders, she had behind her home a dense wood through which Franklin used to play in his youth, a gentle stream not one hundred yards east of the home. Fish were far from insufficient in that stream. Many times Augustus took Franklin there to fish. They caught trout. Sometimes they caught nothing. But Franklin always came back with a smile on his face, sat at the kitchen table after fishing, and had a cup of hot chocolate.

Lying in bed, she thought if Franklin remembered the poems he used to write. He must, she thought. There was shoebox full of old poems he had written. They would comprise a tome if they were put in one book. She had no clue where she had put that shoebox and thought somewhere in this big house was a plethora of childish verse and made a mental note to search the abode for them, to resurrect her son. She could not deny it. Franklin had become a man of honor. But, there was, she realized, this day, a certain innocence lost; a tentativeness that she loved in him was gone. He was full of witticisms and idioms.

Teleportation to better times and better places. Death, youth. It made no difference. People changed and people never did. She was ensconced and so was Franklin by Augustus's death. How ensconced they were there was no telling.

Franklin Tremont searched his pockets for the instruction manual of a one-hundred and eighty watt stereo system, now installed in Judy Tremont's living room. "It's simple," Franklin said, "once you get used to it."

Judy was standing poised, observing Franklin. He was fiddling with the six CD changer. From the garage, he had gotten all her CDs. There were few. Sinatra, Ravel, and of course Piaf. He put in a CD and hit play. Piaf's voice came in over the speakers.

"How's that for sound?" Franklin asked.

Judy stood, apprehensive. She had not listened to music in years.

"The silence would debilitate you," Franklin said.

Judy did not speak. She stood, listened, and shifted her weight one foot to the other and watched Franklin. He was the victor. She had succumbed to his wishes. She did not want the stereo in her house and thought that Augustus and Augustus only was the envoy to happiness.

Franklin stood. "Piaf was debutante."

"I don't know what that means," Judy said.

"Just listen. You know this song."

She did. It was one of her favorite Edith Piaf songs, *"Non, Je Ne Regrette Rien."* She felt like crying. She did not want to cry in front of Franklin. He was so wrapped up in his stereo system. A sham. Augustus's headstone was occupying her thoughts. They bought two adjoining plots at the local cemetery. Augustus was being laid to rest next week. "Franklin, are you coming to the funeral?"

He paused "Non, Je Ne Regrette Rien." "Of course. Trish and the two kids will be there, too."

"Good, because I don't want be alone in a big cold cemetery with Betty Silverman, Rita Purcell, and the priest. I don't want to think you've forgotten us."

Franklin had the intention of buying a bouquet of chartreuse daisies and laying them on the grave. "I wouldn't miss it," he said, and started up the Piaf song again. A precocious wave, compassion, took Franklin to his mother and he held her tight. It was as if he were willing away the apathy, a deportation.

Judy had already picked out the casket, an ebony casket, which would house Augustus. The previous night, she had come to a realization. She wanted nothing of the world. That morning she unhooked her phone. She was not expecting calls. And she did not want absentminded calls from some telemarketer to off-end her meditative train of thought. But, the fear remained with the realization. She yearned for a sense of transparency; a means to elevate. She caught herself the previous night thinking about the emasculation of saints—that was her last thought before sleep—and a feeling, delinquent and apathetic, overcame her upon waking, a feeling that attempted to destroy oscillating memories, Augustus, strong tea and snowfall and warm clothes, the memories actualized and quite captivating.

She had dreamt of villas that morning before waking and titivating chateaus, which danced in her vision like illusions. The finality of seasons, children prancing and birds flocking. Picturesque and taunting, the image stayed for many seconds and she wanted to penetrate into the expanse and dillydally in the garden. Eloquent clouds were vivid in her dream and held substance, as if they could congeal into Godhead and defeat, eviscerate any foe, any villain that came to pass. Judy had met her deadline. Fate was showing her this stable and perfect vision and she made a pact in that dream with herself that she would not tell anybody about it—there was now only the inevitability that she traverse into and evoke within these illustrious memories before they did evaporate.

About the Author

Anders M. Svenning was born in New York. He started writing with seriousness at the age of nineteen and has now been published in many literary magazines throughout the United States and abroad. Some of the most recent include *Dark Gothic Magazine, Adelaide Literary Magazine*, and *Degenerate Literature.* He is the author of *Nonpareil* (Tule Fog Press), *50 States Poetry* (Pansophic Press), and has a collection of short stories forthcoming, titled *Verdant Grounds, Subtle Boundaries* (Adelaide Books). *The Phrenologist* (Wapshott Press), a novella, is also forthcoming piece by Anders M. Svenning. Anders M. Svenning lives in Palm City, Florida.

Publishing Credits

These stories were written between the years 2012 and 2017. All of the stories appear in the order they were published except for the first two stories in the collection. Those two stories remain unpublished by literary magazines but are finding their way into print and online vis a vis the collection you are now holding in your hands, Verdant Grounds, Subtle Boundaries, which was a pleasure to write and publish, and whose pleasure now is all the readers'.

Anders M. Svenning
Palm City, Florida
19 August 2017

(2013) "Ingenuity" Forge Journal Issue 6.3
(2013) "A Beautiful Tyde" Grey Sparrow Review Issue 17
(2015) "Equal Men" Potluck Magazine September
(2015) "On His Way to Elysia" The Rain, Party, & Disaster Society October
(2015) "The Column of Air" The Rain, Party, & Disaster Society

(2015) "Eight Minutes to Thanu" The Kentucky Review Volume 2 February
(2016) "Engine Trouble" The Chicago Record
(2016) "Young Lovers" Feminine Collective March
(2016) "Aurora Sunrise" Futures Trading Magazine Volume 4, Issue 1 May
(2016) "On Death" GTK Creative Magazine Issue 7
(2016) "Apollo's" Conceit Magazine Volume 10
(2016) "Of Interest" The Wagon Magazine
(2017) "In Columbus" Degenerate Literature 16
(2017) "The Beauty in Bereavement" Adelaide Literary Magazine No.9 September Issue

www.ingramcontent.com/pod-product-compliance
Lightning Source LLC
Chambersburg PA
CBHW021018120726
47905CB00009B/3072

* 9 7 8 0 9 9 9 5 1 6 4 0 9 *